By the time she moved in to Tobias's house, her fake engagement had to be fully operational.

Tilting her head back, she gazed at Tobias from beneath her lashes. "Are you trying to tell me that I can't sleep with my fiancé?"

Something dangerous flashed in Tobias's eyes, as if she had finally pushed him over the edge of a precipice she hadn't known was there. Out of nowhere a hot thrill shot down her spine.

"Not in my house," he said softly.

Their gazes locked with a laser intensity she was having difficulty breaking, probably because Tobias's eyes had a magnetic, mesmerizing quality, which, somehow, made all brain function stop.

Approximately ninety seconds ago she had figured out that Tobias wanted her. Now she had another vital piece of information.

He was jealous.

Dear Reader,

Tobias Hunt appeared as "the other guy" in *Twin Scandals*. Dark and dangerous hero material, but with a definite niceness to him, he had dated both of the Messena twins, but seemed content to stay in the friend zone.

Of course I had to write his story and figure out what his problem was! When Southern beauty Allegra Mallory strolled onto the page with her perfect makeup, stylish clothes and quirky ex–beauty queen attitude, I finally got it. Tobias had fallen for her *ages* ago; he just hadn't accepted it...yet.

I hope, in these uncertain times, that you have as much fun reading Tobias and Allegra's story as I had writing it!

Every blessing,

Fiona

FIONA BRAND

HOW TO LIVE WITH
TEMPTATION

Thank you, as always,
to my wonderful editor,
Stacy Boyd.

ISBN-13: 978-1-335-23279-3

How to Live with Temptation

Copyright © 2021 by Fiona Gillibrand

PLEASE RECYCLE
THIS PRODUCT IS RECYCLABLE

Recycling programs
for this product may
not exist in your area.

This edition published by arrangement with Harlequin Books S.A.

For questions and comments about the quality of this book, please contact us at CustomerService@Harlequin.com.

Harlequin Enterprises ULC
22 Adelaide St. West, 40th Floor
Toronto, Ontario M5H 4E3, Canada
www.Harlequin.com

Printed in U.S.A.

Fiona Brand lives in the sunny Bay of Islands, New Zealand. Aside from being a mother to two real-life heroes, her sons, Fiona likes to garden, cook and travel. After a life-changing encounter, she continues to walk with God as she studies toward a bachelor of theology, serves as a priest in the Anglican Church and as a chaplain for the Order of St. Luke, Christ's healing ministry.

Books by Fiona Brand

Harlequin Desire

How to Live with Temptation

The Pearl House

A Breathless Bride
A Tangled Affair
A Perfect Husband
The Fiancée Charade
Just One More Night
Needed: One Convenient Husband
Twin Scandals
Keeping Secrets

Visit her Author Profile page at Harlequin.com for more titles.

You can also find Fiona Brand on Facebook, along with other Harlequin Desire authors, at Facebook.com/harlequindesireauthors.

To the Lord: Father, Son and Holy Spirit. Thank You!

"The Lord bless thee, and keep thee: The Lord make his face shine upon thee, and be gracious unto thee...and give thee peace."

—The Aaronic blessing, *Numbers* 6:24–26

One

Allegra Mallory checked the rearview mirror of her gorgeous new convertible as she made the turn off Miami's Biscayne Boulevard onto Sixth Street. Her heart sped up as the glossy black truck that was following her, and which she was almost certain belonged to billionaire tycoon Tobias Hunt, cruised up behind her.

Tobias. Six foot two inches of grim, muscled male, with wintry gray eyes, cheekbones to die for and a rock-solid jaw. *The man with whom she had spent one passionate night with two years ago.*

Irritation, and a tension she had no interest in identifying, made her fingers tense on the steering wheel. The last time she had seen Tobias had been at her great-aunt Esmae's funeral just days ago. It went without saying that she had avoided him, which had been easy because a great many people had attended the church service, and then afterward had filled Esmae's beautiful old Hacienda-style beach mansion. However, when her aunt's lawyer's office had called to give her a time for the reading of the will, which would also be attended by Tobias, who happened to be Esmae's step-grandson, avoidance was no longer an option.

Allegra braked for a set of lights. Another glance in her rearview mirror confirmed that he was still on her tail and, out of nowhere, unwilling memories surfaced.

The fact that she had done the one thing she had always promised herself she would never do, have a one-night stand, *and with the last man on the planet she should ever have gone near*, still annoyed her.

Not that she had thought it would be a one-night stand.

At the time, she had been silly enough to think that, because she'd had a crush on Tobias for the last four years, *he was the one* for her, and that this could be the beginning of something deep and real. The kind of relationship her parents had, and which she had always thought would automatically fall into her lap because she was a good person and absolutely deserved to be loved.

The black truck nosed in close behind her in the gridlocked traffic, further dwarfing her car and making her feel distinctly herded. Allegra frowned at the tinted windows that obscured the identity of the driver but, before the truck had gotten too close, she had caught a glimpse of the license plate in her rearview mirror. The legend, *Hunts*—wordplay on Hunt Security—had made her stomach tighten and sent a sharp, unwanted little thrill down her spine.

Not that Tobias was hunting her, she thought firmly. Normally, they were very good at avoiding each other. The only reason he was behind her was that they were both driving to the same place, because they both had to be at the reading of Esmae's will.

Unable to resist, Allegra glanced in her rearview mirror yet again. This time she caught movement and the flash of Miami's hot, morning sun glinting off dark glasses. Another sharp little zing went through her, because Tobias was now looking directly at her, which meant he knew she had been checking him out.

Suddenly aware of how visible she was in her convertible, while Tobias was concealed behind the badass gangster glass, she looked doggedly ahead at the sea of midmorning traffic.

The tension that was still gripping her, and the odd little darts of adrenaline, were simply a product of having to deal with Tobias after the grief of losing Esmae, and her natural apprehension about the will. One thing was certain: she was *not* attracted to Tobias, and she definitely wasn't turned on by him.

Following their one night together, and the fact that, just a few days later, Tobias had been photographed with gorgeous heiress Francesca Messena, her mom—worried that the rejection was making her actually feel *inadequate*—had paid for her to get some professional counseling. To complete her healing, Allegra had also signed up for a number of alternative therapies to purge the memories and release her anger.

One of those therapies, centered on forgiveness, had involved writing forgiveness statements and burning them. The politically correct words had been difficult to write, but the flames had been fun. By the time she had finished, she had also succeeded in doing some helpful research for her spa business, and she had achieved her goal: she was no longer attracted to Tobias.

The light turned green. Allegra accelerated smoothly through the intersection, enjoying the purr of the car's engine while she tried to concentrate on following the verbal instructions of her navigational system, which was speaking to her in a distractingly sexy British accent. Problem was, she enjoyed listening to the deep, male voice so much, she kept forgetting the instructions. Luckily, she had twenty-twenty vision and saw the turn she needed to make directly ahead. Seconds later, she swung into the underground parking garage of the high-rise that housed Esmae's lawyer's ultra-expensive law firm.

Aware that Tobias was, once more, practically tail to bumper with her, she braked at the barrier to take her ticket then accelerated just a little too fast in the vast, dungeon-like lot as she began looking for a space. Because it was downtown and midmorning, and the building contained a busy events center, of course, it was packed.

Allegra caught movement off to the right. She didn't know if a vehicle had gone into a space or was leaving but, on the off chance that it was exiting, she took a right hand turn into the next lane. The payoff for that was that Tobias cruised on straight ahead, so he was no longer tailing her.

But Allegra's relief was short-lived because, seconds later, a pretty woman and her young daughter, who was dressed in a hot-pink leotard, her hair piled on top of her head and glittering with diamantés, exited the car, which had obviously just parked.

On the drive in she had seen the billboards advertising the junior beauty pageant that was taking place at the center, so it was a good bet that the little girl was a contestant. The pretty picture the little girl made spun her back to her days on the beauty pageant circuit, which she had quit when she was sixteen, mostly because she refused to wear pink and rhinestones: not even if she was dead. And if anyone dressed her in pink and rhinestones when she was dead, she would come back to haunt them.

But then her mother had dangled a collegiate pageant that was offering a chunk of cash that would go a long way toward her university costs, plus a car and diamonds. Allegra had mulled it over for a whole five seconds. Should she go for it?

Does a hungry lion lunge at a steak?

In the end it had been a no-brainer, so she had gotten the cash, the car *and* the diamonds. She wasn't so hot on the silver-and-crystal crown, but on down days, sometimes it was nice to wear it.

Frustrated at the seemingly full parking garage, but relentlessly positive, she continued searching for a spot. Her mother, at this point, would ask God to get her a parking space, but that was where she and her mother parted company. Paige Mallory was the pampered only daughter of an old Louisiana family, the Toussaints, an ex–Miss Louisiana beauty queen and a real piece of work. The way Allegra saw it, God was way too busy fixing the mess people had made of the world to park her car for her, so she lifted that burden from His shoulders and did it herself.

There would be a space in here; the ticketing machine wouldn't have let her in otherwise.

She just had to find it before Tobias did.

When she was almost at the end of the lane, she caught the glow of taillights down to the right. Since she didn't think any new cars had entered the building in the last few seconds, that could only mean someone was leaving. At the same time, she caught a second flash of movement off to the left. She frowned. Tobias had also noticed that the car was leaving, and now his muscular black truck was heading straight for the space.

Adrenaline pumped. She came from a family where rules were rules and manners were important. Her father and her four older brothers opened doors for women. Invitations were sent in the mail, not texted; dinner was eaten at a table, with cloth napkins; and important conversations were conducted in a civilized way, face-to-face.

She should do the right thing, wait politely and let him take the space.

But two years ago, Tobias had not done the right thing by her. He had turned their night of passion into a meaningless encounter, then, a couple of days later, had made it even more meaningless by breaking up with her *over the phone*.

Her jaw tightened.

Then, before she could veto the action, her foot jammed down on the accelerator.

Tobias Hunt braked hard as a white convertible, with the name *Madison Spas* emblazoned across its side, made a fast turn out of the lane just ahead, cutting him off then slotting neatly into *his* space.

Even if he hadn't recognized the showy white convertible as he'd driven into town, he would had to have been blind not to recognize the distinctive head of silky chestnut hair piled into a messy knot, the delicate cheekbones and faintly imperious nose half-hidden by a pair of oversize sunglasses.

Allegra Mallory.

A former beauty queen, tagged by prominent social media influencer Buffy Hamilton in her list of "Who's Going to Marry a Billionaire," at a hot #2, right behind Buffy, who had listed herself at #1.

Maybe that isn't a piece of information that a burned-out-Special-Forces-operative-turned-CEO-of-a-security-conglomerate should know, he thought bleakly, but it was a fact that he'd had significant encounters with both women.

Buffy, clearly intrigued by his rise into the billionaire stratosphere six months ago, when his family trust had finally released his inheritance, had invited him aboard her father's luxurious yacht. He had declined the weekend party for two.

In stark contrast, Allegra, who had strolled into his life six years ago, had never invited him anywhere. All she'd had to do was arrive in Miami with her cool dark gaze, rich list style and Southern stroll to utterly disrupt his life.

As he cruised past, Tobias caught a glimpse of long tanned legs and sexy high heels as Allegra stepped from the car. The sharp visual of her in an emerald green dress and snazzy little jacket that clung to her figure and provided a tantalizing hint of shadowy cleavage, nixed his frustration that he was now going to be late for the reading of Esmae's will.

Jaw taut, he attempted to clamp down on the now-all-too-familiar sharpening masculine interest and the humming tension that Allegra always inspired, as if an electrical current was coursing through his body.

For over half a decade he had worked hard to suppress the potent attraction that had blindsided him when Esmae's niece had first arrived in Miami, just weeks after he had moved in with his longtime girlfriend, Lindsay. An attraction that still seemed as disruptive and all-consuming as it had two years ago when, after breaking up with Lindsay, *because he couldn't forget Allegra*, he had finally given in to temptation and spent one passionate night with her.

In doing so, he had been aware that he had crossed a line. He had become like the father he had spent most of his life trying to forget.

James Hunt hadn't been able to settle into either a good marriage or a bad affair. He had destroyed Tobias's mother's life by leaving her alone and dangling, while he had moved from liaison to liaison with a never-ending string of A-list party girls. Fifteen years ago, he had finally died in a car accident, leaving them to pick up the pieces. Although, it hadn't been soon enough for Alicia Hunt, who had developed a heart condition and passed away just six months later.

Tobias had read the medical reports; he knew the jargon, but that didn't change the fact that his mother had died of a broken heart.

He continued to cruise, but memories of that night kept distracting him from his search for another parking space.

A clear, hot night, the sky brilliant with stars, the French doors of Esmae's beach house flung wide to admit the cooling sea breeze. The sound of waves breaking on the shore, and Allegra Mallory, even more gorgeous naked, sleeping like a baby in the rumpled bed they had shared.

Fingers tensing on the steering wheel, he dismissed the too-vivid images that reminded him that he had done the one thing he had promised himself he wouldn't do. He had stepped into the well-worn tradition of Hunt men, thrown away the rock-solid relationship he had committed to and gone after a glitzy socialite on the make.

And the mistake he had made had had repercussions that still haunted him, because Lindsay, unbeknown to either of them, had been pregnant. As it turned out, she had lost the baby the day after he had slept with Allegra. Although she had been at pains to absolve him of guilt, Tobias was acutely aware that if he had stayed with Lindsay, if he had ignored the attraction to Allegra, the baby, *his child*, might have lived.

Two years ago, weighed down with guilt, sick to his stomach at the damage he had caused, he had controlled the desire to plunge into a liaison with Allegra that he was well aware could only be based on the magnetic pull of the Hunt billions, and had cut all ties. Their one night together was old history. What really concerned him now was the fact that she was here for the reading of the will.

She was here to collect.

An incoming call distracted him from brooding on exactly what Hunt possessions Esmae had left to her only niece. Tapping the glowing icon on the truck's touch screen, he answered the call from his ex-military buddy, JT. "I know I'm late," he growled. "My flight was delayed. Stall Phillips until I get there."

Damned if he would miss any part of this meeting. Esmae had held shares in Hunt Security. With five percent of the multibillion-dollar firm his family had painstakingly built from nothing up for grabs, and the aristocratic Mallory family's notorious history of swindling and conning his once-dirt-poor family, it was a no-brainer. He had to be there.

JT didn't bother to hide his impatience. "You don't seriously think Esmae left the shares to Allegra? After all, they are *Hunt* shares—"

"That fell into Esmae's hands, because my grandfather neglected to make a new will after he married her, then had the bad luck to die suddenly in a boating accident."

But the real slippery dealing had gone back a generation further than that, to his great-grandfather Jebediah, who had once worked as a ranch hand for Alexandra Mallory until he had gone shares with her in a land purchase. Three years later, in the middle of a drought, and a hot affair with Jebediah, Alexandra had disappeared into the sunset. The lawyer who had cut the ranch in half had somehow managed to give Alexandra the piece that, soon after, became one of the richest oil fields in Texas. Meanwhile, Tobias's family had ended up with a dust bowl that had almost driven them broke.

He clamped down on his impatience. JT was a shark but, as long as their friendship was, he was a newcomer to the firm and hadn't had time to absorb all of the nuances of the Hunt/Mallory saga. "If Esmae was going to play nice with the shares, she would have accepted my father's offer to buy them twenty years ago, but she refused. The only saving grace was that my grandfather had the foresight to sign over ninety-five percent of the business to my father a couple of years before he died, otherwise Hunt Securities would be Mallory Securities."

"But Esmae did give you an undertaking before she died—"

"That was when I was the only beneficiary of Esmae's will. Then, two years ago, Allegra moved to Miami full-time, the will got changed and Esmae decided to keep the new will under wraps." Tobias's gaze broodingly skimmed the ranks of cars. "Esmae made changes she knew I wasn't going to like. Why else keep them a secret?"

His pulse rate lifted as he caught a glimpse of Allegra stepping into an elevator. Her head turned; her gaze clashed with his. A split second later, the doors closed, and the fiction that she hadn't noticed she had cut him off and stolen his parking spot died a death.

Tobias negotiated another tight turn and took the ramp up to the next level, which looked as packed as the one he had left. "The Hunt Security shares should come to me," Tobias said bleakly "but it's a fact that I'm not blood kin to Esmae, and Allegra Mallory is. And, when a Mallory is in the picture, all bets are off."

His great-grandfather Jebediah had known that better than anyone. "Don't forget, Esmae bankrolled Allegra's spa business, and it's a fact that Allegra has been at Esmae's bedside for a good few months now."

There was a small silence. "You really think Allegra's likely to pull something like that? I've read the online hype, but, hey, let's remember who's writing it. Buffy Hamilton. I mean, *seriously*...?"

Tobias found himself controlling his temper with difficulty, which was unusual, because he never lost his cool, and especially not with JT. They'd spent a tour of duty in Afghanistan together. If there was one person he trusted to have his back, it was JT. "You dated Buffy, so I guess you should know."

"You're beginning to sound like Julia. I spent a weekend on her father's yacht," JT muttered. "There's a difference."

Julia was the girlfriend with whom JT had recently broken up. Tobias frowned. "You didn't tell me that was the reason for the breakup."

"It wasn't. Let's just say there were...other factors, but Julia managed to bring Buffy into the picture."

"You mean there *was* someone else."

Which was no surprise. JT was tall, tanned and blond, with the kind of muscular beach-boy good looks women seemed to find irresistible. He was also the son of a mega-rich Florida real estate tycoon, so he had no lack of "next" girlfriends.

"Not...exactly. My point is that the *someone else* I was interested in wasn't Buffy."

"Back to the will," Tobias said flatly. "Six months ago, Esmae made Allegra a beneficiary of her *secret* will. That means Esmae's done something I'm not going to like, and whatever it is, Allegra's in it up to her neck."

"I get it that Esmae's been secretive. I just don't

think Allegra's the type to leverage benefits from a dying relative."

Tobias stiffened. The last time he had discussed the will with JT, they had been on the same page. Now, it sounded like JT had joined the Allegra Mallory fan club. "I didn't know you'd met Allegra." *And fallen under her spell.*

There was a brief silence. "As it happens, we, uh, did meet a couple of times. Julia was a client at her spa, used to swear by her herbal wraps and mud baths. And we might have had her over for dinner along with some other friends."

Tobias's jaw tightened. That was an "affirmative" on JT falling under Allegra's spell.

He gave up on the upper-level parking and cruised back down to the lower deck, scanned the rows of cars and finally caught some movement. "I'm guessing that was before you split with Julia."

There was a small, stiff silence. "I'm hardly likely to have had Allegra over for dinner otherwise."

"No," Tobias said softly, "because that would be a date."

JT and Julia had split up a month ago. Tobias now had to wonder if Allegra was the reason JT's relationship had foundered. If she was running true to the online hype, she could be angling for JT to be her next wealthy lover.

Grimly, he accelerated toward the area he had seen the car leaving. "There's only one reason I asked you to be present at the reading of the will, and that's because something's up. I wouldn't have needed you, otherwise. I'll see you in a few minutes."

Tobias terminated the call.

JT and Allegra. He had not seen that coming.

And it would be happening over his dead body.

As luck would have it, the vacant space was just two down from where Allegra's stylish convertible was parked.

He checked his watch. His annoyance shot up another notch when he noted that he was now a good ten minutes late. Exiting the truck, he locked it, strode toward the elevators and punched in the number of the floor. As the elevator sped upward, he remembered the last interview he'd had with Esmae, who, even at ninety-two, had been strong-willed, imperious and just a tad manipulative.

All recognizable Mallory traits.

From odd things his step-grandmother had let drop, Tobias knew that Esmae had done something out of the ordinary with the will. The fact that she had kept it secret, and that he had not had access to a copy of it, was the final confirmation.

Allegra's presence at the reading guaranteed that the changes involved Esmae's great-niece.

The doors slid open. He strode into the plush offices of Esmae's lawyer's law firm and was directed to her lawyer Phillips's office. As he stepped through the door, his gaze automatically settled on Allegra. Her dark glance clashed with his. Despite bracing himself for the moment, every muscle in his body tightened.

Not for the first time it occurred to him that, usually with women, he could walk away clean. When it was over, it was over. But when it came to Allegra, the usual rules hadn't applied.

Neither had time and distance, or the guilt that had gnawed at him, worked their magic. Despite searching out and dating other women who should have been perfect for him, just as his ex Lindsay had been, he still wanted Allegra Mallory.

Join the club with who-knew-how-many other men, including JT.

A little grimly, he refreshed himself on the past record of Mallory and Hunt liaisons.

Alexandra Mallory had slept with Jebediah, then scammed him, making herself even richer in the process. That was strike one.

Seventy years ago, Esmae had escaped the financial crash that had nixed the fabled Mallory fortune and solved the family's poverty problem by jumping on his grandfather Michael Hunt's newly minted money train. Strike two.

Esmae had been beautiful, but Allegra, with her rich hair, delicately molded cheekbones, firm jaw and wide mouth, was next-level gorgeous.

Even so, there was no way in hell he was going to let Allegra Mallory carry on the family tradition with him.

There was not going to be a strike three.

Two

Allegra dragged her gaze from the brooding, magnetic challenge of Tobias's, as if in taking the parking space *he* had wanted, and making him a good fifteen minutes late for the appointment, she had thrown down a gauntlet.

And he had picked it up.

Guilt that she had behaved so aggressively, and other less distinct and more disturbing sensations that coiled in the pit of her stomach, was almost instantly replaced by fiery irritation. She couldn't help thinking that it was not a bad thing that, for once in his life, Tobias hadn't gotten something he wanted just because he had wanted it.

Taking a measured breath, she smoothed out her expression. But maintaining any level of calm was difficult, because when Tobias stepped into the room, with his broad shoulders, cool gray gaze and that palpable air of command, he took up all the air.

Her fingers automatically went to the simple-but-classy diamond bracelet at her wrist, which had been part of that last prize package she had won as a beauty queen. Wearing the diamonds had been a conscious choice for this meeting, not just because diamonds went with *everything*, but because the jewelry reminded her that she was successful and goal oriented, and that her life was not defined by others' mistakes.

And, it was a fact that in the last two and a half years, following a fake scandal that had ended the high-flying business career in San Francisco that she had sweated blood to attain, she'd had to forgive a lot of those kinds of mistakes.

Determinedly ignoring Tobias and his smooth-talking lawyer, JT, she directed a cool glance at Phillips. "Perhaps we should start? I have an appointment at twelve that I don't want to miss."

The appointment was with a funky little vegan café that made her favorite herb-and-nut salad, and chocolate bliss balls that were to die for, but no one here needed to know that.

"And we wouldn't want you to be late," Tobias said in a soft, curt voice that made her stomach clench.

Doing her best to control the flush that warmed her cheeks, Allegra kept her gaze firmly on Phillips, who was looking at her in a measuring way as he handed her a copy of the will. After six months with a finance firm that had seemed filled with men who, apparently, hadn't yet grasped that women could look attractive and still have schedules and priorities that did not include them, she had gotten used to that look.

Apparently, because she had inherited the chestnut Mallory hair and her mother's dark eyes and traffic-stopping figure, men found it difficult to take her seriously. That was their problem, totally, but she was a helpful person and usually, in a business setting, she did her best to tone down her appearance.

However, today, with Tobias in the mix, she hadn't been inclined to tone down *anything.* The dress she was wearing discreetly hugged her curves, revealed a hint of cleavage and was short enough to showcase her long legs, which were possibly her best feature. The matching bolero jacket gave the outfit a more business feel while at the same time emphasizing the way the dress cinched in at her waist and that her bust size—courtesy of her mom—was a "don't mess with me" 36C.

Instead of a sophisticated French pleat, she had gone for a looser, messier knot, which looked great with a pair of diamond Chanel earrings that had been a graduation gift from her father. As a gift, the earrings had been a little over-the-top. Her brothers had been annoyed because they had only gotten watches, but what could she say? She was Daddy's girl.

In any case, the dress and the jacket—besides giving her the pampered, high-end look she needed in her business—were by the newest, hottest designer in the business: Francesca Messena.

Maybe it might seem strange that she would wear clothing made and designed by the woman she had learned had slept with Tobias both before *and* after he had slept with her. But the way Allegra saw it, buying Francesca's clothing was a clear sign that she had healed and moved on, and that the stinging sense of betrayal when Tobias had ditched her in favor of Francesca had been utterly banished from her psyche.

And, of course, it went without saying that, as part of her recovery process, she had forgiven Francesca. It had taken a while—she had burned a whole ream of forgiveness statements before the job got done—but she had kept reminding herself that Francesca was basically a good person. She simply hadn't known how big a rat Tobias was. Besides, why should she be denied the clothes she wanted to wear just because Tobias had been briefly included in both of their lives?

To not wear the Messena brand was to say that Allegra lived in a universe where Tobias controlled what she did and did not wear, and last she heard, Tobias was *not* the ruler of the universe.

As Phillips started reading, Allegra skimmed the first page, aware that, somewhere within the document, there was going to be a surprise she was not going to like. That surprise could only have to do with Madison Spas, because the only reason she was here was that Esmae held fifty percent of the shares.

Too late to wish she hadn't let her aunt invest, and that she had done what she had originally planned and taken out a loan with her own bank.

Just four months ago, when Allegra had learned Esmae was terminal, she had even offered to buy out the shares, but Esmae had said there was no need, since she was leaving them to Allegra in her will. That would have been all well and good, except that Esmae had then point-blank refused to let Allegra see a copy of the will.

Now she was braced for a worst-case scenario. She could be about to lose control of the business she had started, and which she loved with passion, to Tobias Hunt!

Extracting her reading glasses from her handbag, she slipped them on and attempted to concentrate on the legalese. Normally, she was very good at speed-reading and picking out the main points, courtesy of a master's degree in finance, but with Tobias pacing Phillips's overlarge office like a large, caged cat, it was difficult to concentrate.

By the third page in, she was beginning to relax, then Phillips delivered the kind of punch line that had her rereading the clause.

Live in Esmae's beach mansion, for a whole month with Tobias, or she would lose the shares in her business?

She went hot, then cold, then hot again. She reread the clause, just in case there had been a mistake.

There wasn't, and in that moment, a mistake *she* had made came back to haunt her.

After spending that one night with Tobias, she had been indiscreet enough to tell Esmae what had happened. The words had practically burst out of her because she had been so confident that she was on the brink of the kind of deep, life-altering relationship with Tobias that she had secretly hoped would be in her future.

Predictably, Esmae had been reserved. Even though she had married a Hunt, she knew that if there was one man Allegra shouldn't have slept with, it was Tobias, because the acrimony that had existed between the Hunts and the Mallorys for a good three generations was, apparently, still alive and well.

Too late to regret telling Esmae her deepest, darkest secret. A secret her aunt had promised not to tell.

Now, it was suddenly looking like the past wasn't buried after all, because it seemed that Esmae was attempting to matchmake from beyond the grave.

Of course, there was a thin possibility that this might not be about matchmaking. Esmae, the only Mallory who had ever actually married a Hunt—a second marriage to Tobias's grandfather—could simply be trying to help the two families reconcile their differences. Although that didn't make sense since, now that Esmae was gone, there was literally nothing to tie the two families together.

Allegra frowned. Two years ago, when she had confided in Esmae, had she been silly enough to speculate that marriage might be in their future?

An embarrassing, too-vivid memory surfaced. That would be a *yes* on mentioning the marriage word.

She drew an impeded breath, abruptly aware that Tobias was standing, arms folded across his chest, gunmetal-gray eyes trained on her, as if he believed the "living together" clause had been her handiwork.

As if she had manipulated Esmae into changing the will because she still wanted Tobias.

A slow, deep flush warmed her cheeks. *As if.*

JT, whom she knew on a casual basis because his ex-girlfriend Julia used to be a regular client at Madison Spas, seemed more relaxed, but there was no mistaking the same cold, incisive gaze.

Mortification aside, the combined presence of Tobias and JT, in theory, should have made her feel embattled, like a small animal cornered by a powerful and efficient wolf pack. But it was a fact that she had grown up with four very large older brothers and, by the time she had turned five, that tactic hadn't worked for them, either.

Taking a deep breath, Allegra forced herself to relax. She was doing exactly what her therapist had advised her not to do: overstressing. The problem was she liked to be in control, and ever since Esmae had died, everything had been distinctly out of control.

She took another slow, deep breath and closed her eyes for just a second as she attempted to center herself by using a visualization recommended by her Christian meditation instructor. Unfortunately, the calming image of a limpid, moonlit lake seemed to have developed a roiling whirlpool right at the center.

Her lids flickered open; Tobias's gaze locked

with hers before dropping to her mouth. Another one of those stomach-clenching electrical tingles ran through her, as if, deep down, at some primitive level, her body couldn't help but respond to Tobias.

But that couldn't be, she thought, briskly, since she was over him. They were *over one another*.

It would be a chilly day in hell before either of them would willingly choose to share personal space.

Although, it was looking like there was no way to avoid it.

Tobias said something short and flat under his breath, "So, there's no way out of this."

Annoyed at the way his statement mirrored her own thought, her gaze clashed with his again, which was a mistake, because another jolt of tingling heat set her even more on edge.

Tobias moved so that his broad shoulders blocked a good deal of the hot sun streaming through the window of Phillips's office. He pinned Phillips with that remote, unnerving gaze, and suddenly the stories about Tobias's time in the military as some kind of Special Forces ghost seemed to gather force.

"Let me get this right. If I don't share the house with Allegra, I lose shares in *my* business."

The edge to Tobias's statement underlined his annoyance that there was a lot more at stake for him than for Allegra, courtesy of the fact that he was the CEO of a multibillion-dollar security firm. She was also aware that the shares that Tobias's grandfather had left to Esmae several years ago weren't just ordinary shares, they were a crucial chunk of voting shares. That meant that whoever held them had the right to vote on matters of corporate policy.

She had no idea how much they would be worth. Although, given Tobias's bread-and-butter security products like house and car alarms, his extremely expensive detective agency and VIP security service, and other whispers about military contracts and satellites, she guessed the figure could be in the millions.

Phillips, who had an ex-military look himself, with a short crisp haircut and a square jaw, flipped a page, as if he had to refresh himself on the type of clause that no lawyer was likely to forget. "That's correct."

Allegra coolly redirected Phillips's attention back to her. "And if I don't live in my great-aunt's house for a month, I'll lose shares in *my* business to Tobias?" She wasn't worth millions, or even billions like Tobias. Her net worth was more in the six figures range, if you counted her mortgage, but even so… "Madison Spas is important to me, and it's not, exactly, worth peanuts—"

Philips gave her the kind of politely disbelieving look that signaled that, at some point in the proceedings, he had joined Tobias's wolf pack. "The terms set for both sets of shares are there in black-and-white Miss Mallory, clause 16 C."

Tobias, who had moved to prop himself on the edge of the lawyer's enormous mahogany desk, crossed his arms over his chest. "I'm not exactly interested in picking up shares in your beauty business—"

"It's *not* a beauty salon." Aware that her voice was just a little too clipped, she forced herself to do a silent count to five.

When it came to dealing with strong alpha males like Tobias, responding in emotional ways was a complete waste of time. Knowledge and logic were what counted but, according to her mother, there was another, even more effective, tactic. It contained no logic whatsoever: you just looked for an opportunity to say *no*.

She met Tobias's gaze squarely and tried to ignore the fact that his expensive masculine cologne was having an annoyingly distracting effect on her. "As I'm sure you know, Madison Spas is an exclusive spa and retreat center specializing in de-stressing therapies and holistic living."

"Which is exactly my point. It's not, exactly, my line of business."

"I'm glad you made that point," Allegra said smoothly, "because producing homogenous boxes of car alarms and door locks doesn't exactly interest me, either."

There was a brief silence. "Hunt Security does more than make locks and alarms."

"Oh, I forgot…you also have some kind of a detective agency."

JT made a muffled sound, somewhere between a cough and a laugh.

A gleam of something close to amusement surfaced in Tobias's gaze. "I guess that's one way of describing Hunt Private Investigations."

Allegra suddenly realized that fighting with Tobias was just a little too...exhilarating. The last thing she needed was to open the door on a dangerously addictive attraction that was officially stone-dead.

She sent him a chilly smile. Tobias might be rich and powerful now, but her family, despite being cash-strapped for the last couple of generations, had once been wealthy and successful, too.

JT, who, until that moment, hadn't taken any part in the conversation, caught her eye, which was startling, because for the past twenty minutes, despite the fact that he had been quite friendly to her in the past, he had studiously ignored her. "Maybe you should give Allegra a break, Tobias. You know what Esmae was like...headstrong, unpredictable—"

"If you're trying to suggest Esmae might have had dementia," Phillips interceded, "forget it. She had a test just a few months ago to confirm that she was of sound mind, just in case anyone tried to overturn the will."

JT frowned. "If she didn't have dementia, why write a will like that?"

Allegra didn't miss the implication. If Esmae was of sound mind, then someone else had to have applied pressure on her to write those crazy, eccentric clauses into the will. And, since Tobias would never willingly choose to share a house with her, of course, she had to be the culprit.

Over the innuendoes and veiled insults, she returned her glasses to their case and tucked it in her bag, then rose smoothly to her feet. If there was ever a time to deploy her mother's "no" tactic, and get some power back, this was it. "Contrary to what you all seem to believe, I don't know what on earth possessed my aunt to put that clause in the will, because she *knew* chapter and verse that I'd rather be stranded on a desert island than spend one night under the same roof as Tobias."

She shot Tobias a chilly look, just to make sure he had gotten the *no* message. That not only that she didn't want him, but that she would *never* want him. "Literally, wild horses couldn't drag me. Ever."

A heated, distinctly sexual tingle shot through her when she noted that his gaze was narrowed and glittering and fixed on hers. As if somehow her complete denial had had the complete opposite effect she had intended. That instead of being offended, he had *liked* what she had said.

As if her total, utter rejection had turned him on.

Three

Tobias frowned. "If Esmae knew there was no point putting us in the same house together, why bother?"

It was the wrong question to ask. Two years ago, Allegra had been vulnerable and off-balance after what had happened in San Francisco, and too trusting of Tobias. Now, she was older, smarter and a whole lot more ticked off. "Maybe Esmae put that clause in her will for your sake, not mine."

He folded his arms across his chest. "Okay, I'll play. Why did Esmae think I needed to live with you for a month?"

"Francesca Messena," she said succinctly. "And her twin, Sophie…although, not so much."

It occurred to her that Francesca Messena had been relaxed, vivacious, the kind of woman men were naturally drawn to and loved to date. On the other hand, Sophie had had a reputation for being distant and controlled, more interested in business than men. *More like herself.*

The sudden thought that Tobias had never truly been attracted to her because, like Sophie Messena, she was *not his type*, made her feel even more annoyed. If she was not Tobias's type, that meant the one-night stand they had shared had been even more meaningless than she had thought.

Tobias pinched his nose. "Why are we talking about the Messena twins?"

Jaw tight at the conclusion she had just drawn, that Tobias had slept with her without even liking who she was, Allegra plowed on. "Do I have to paint a picture? You pursued both of the Messena twins—"

"I wouldn't call it pursued, exactly."

"We can split hairs all day long," she said coolly, "but the point is that, just a few months ago, both sisters got hitched in a double wedding to *other* men."

"I recall the wedding, since I was a guest."

"Which is exactly what I'm getting at. Not to put too fine a point on it, but Esmae knew that your love life had, shall we say, hit a downward slope. Clearly she was concerned that you were having trouble finding someone—"

"So she decided to give me a little help."

She rewarded Tobias with the same kind of professional smile she gave her spa clients when they reached a fitness milestone. "Just a theory."

Phillips cleared his throat, the noise punctuating

the tense silence that had descended on the room. "As riveting as all of this is, you can't leave yet, Miss Mallory. There's, uh…more."

Allegra blinked, for a moment she had been so consumed with correcting Tobias that she had forgotten about the will. Even worse, she had done the one thing she had promised herself she would not do—she had become emotional.

Adrenaline still humming through her veins, she sat down.

Almost immediately, Phillips began working his way through the fine print of the will, dealing with special bequests. The Hunt jewelry, apparently a massive haul of soulless diamonds that were kept in a bank vault, went to Tobias. When Phillips mentioned a box of Mallory keepsakes, and a painting of Alexandra Mallory, Esmae's mother and Allegra's great-grandmother, she frowned.

She hadn't known a painting existed. Neither had she thought anything was left of Alexandra's life, because the family fortune had been wiped out. "Are these keepsakes also in the bank vaults?"

Phillips consulted a separate page sitting on his desk. "No, they're not. I assume the items are memorabilia and of no particular value, because your aunt stored them in the attic of the beach house."

As fascinating as it was to hear that Esmae, who had been Alexandra's only daughter, had preserved some memorabilia, the final dry clause made her stiffen.

Esmae had, of course, left her five-star resort, the

luxurious Ocean Beach Resort, which she had built
with Hunt money, to Tobias, with a catch. Unless he
personally managed it for the first month, *the exact
time she and Tobias had to share the beach mansion*,
ownership, in full, was transferred to her.

For a moment, Allegra was too stunned to react.
The "living together" clause had made it look like
she was trying to trap Tobias into marriage; this one
made her look like a scheming gold digger on the
make.

She was abruptly spun back two and a half years,
to the moment her financial career had crashed and
burned because two executives at the firm she had
just started at had both accused her of trying to trade
sex for money, promotions and even jewelry, and all
because she had gotten tired of the usual singles dating scene and had made the fatal mistake of trying
an online, "executive" dating site.

Admittedly, she had dated one of them, Halliday,
once. She hadn't known that he was an executive of
the firm that had employed her, because he had been
away from the San Francisco office for a number of
weeks setting up the new San Diego branch, *and* he
had been using a fake name. Even though he was
married, *to the boss's daughter*, he had been trolling
online, pretending to be single. Annoyed when she
had uncovered his true identity and then had said an
absolute *no* to an office affair, he had then made a
preemptive strike to protect his career and his marriage by claiming on social media that she had offered to sleep with him to get a promotion.

If that wasn't bad enough, another executive of the same firm, Fischer, a close friend of Halliday's, and a nephew of one of the partners, who was also married and using the same dating site, had then cornered her and propositioned her in her office. When he had refused to take *no* for an answer, because, apparently the fact that she was an ex-beauty queen meant that *no* didn't mean *no*, she had been forced to fend him off with a large stapler.

Unfortunately, the glancing blow to his jaw had left a bruise and drawn blood from his lip. To make matters worse, he had reeled back, tripped over a chair and ended up on the floor. At that point, maybe he would have slunk away and said nothing, but another new intern had walked in on them. Face red with embarrassment, Fischer had stormed out, then proceeded to also smear her online, claiming that she had attempted to seduce him and had wanted expensive jewelry in payment.

As a result, she had been hauled before the firm's disciplinary committee. Even though their findings had been "inconclusive," *because there was no evidence*, apparently the scandal had made her position at the firm a "problem." She was pretty sure the "problem" part of her employment had been locked in when she had used the forum to give the managing partners a piece of her mind.

Maybe she should have zipped it, but she didn't like injustice, and the reluctance of her bosses to actually investigate, because of nepotism, had been the last straw. If they lied and covered up for their own executives, she could not recommend that anyone trust their money to them. Using that same logic, she could no longer entrust her career and her talents to them, either, so she quit.

Unfortunately, her victorious exit had been somewhat marred by the manifestation of a mysterious medical condition called SVT, supraventricular tachycardia. That was a complicated term for the fact that, every once in a blue moon, her heart would pound out of control and, if it didn't naturally regulate itself, she needed medical intervention to bring it back to its normal rate. It was a condition that had started up when she had been in college and which her doctor had told her was probably due to the fact that she was a type A personality. In layman's terms that meant she had control-freak tendencies and didn't handle stress well.

She registered that Tobias had said something short and flat, and that JT was lodging his protest with Phillips in succinct lawyer-speak. But, in that moment, she wasn't concerned about either Phillips or JT.

Her gaze clashed with Tobias's. "There's a simple solution. I'll get *my* lawyer to draw up a document that relinquishes all rights—"

"Take a look at clause C," he said. "If you give up your rights to the hotel, and then if I fail to manage it for the next month, it goes to the eldest of your next of kin who is, I believe, your brother, Quin."

She read the next clause, and her stomach sank. There was no way Quin, who already owned a very successful boutique hotel in New Orleans, would release Tobias from the clause. He would take the Ocean Beach Resort in a New York minute.

She fixed Tobias with a level look. "I have no idea what's going on here. The only conversation Esmae and I had was about the shares she held in Madison Spas, and that was because I wanted to buy her out four months ago—"

"So the whole thing about living together wasn't your idea?"

She froze in the middle of refolding the will. "Hmmm, let me see… Go and live in an isolated, overstuffed mansion with the last man on earth I would ever want to share any personal space with?"

She rose to her feet, hooked the strap of her handbag over her shoulder and checked the sleek white smartwatch that encircled her wrist, which indicated she had missed an incoming call from Janice, her receptionist. "That would be no, and no."

Tobias didn't bother to hide his disbelief. "In other words, Esmae thought this up all by herself?"

"Yes." Out of nowhere, her heart began to pound and her stomach tightened around a cold, hard lump of dread that, once again, her reputation was going to be shredded for something she hadn't done. That the lies and deceit that had destroyed her financial career would somehow taint her new business enterprise and destroy that, too.

Although, that wasn't likely to happen, she thought crisply. She was her own boss. This time no one could pressure her to leave.

Although, Tobias could refuse to renew her lease.

That would create difficulties, because she would have to relocate the spa. She was currently looking at new premises for a second spa, but that would take months to set up. If she had to move the business in the next few weeks, she wouldn't have anywhere to go.

Taking a calming breath, she did a slow, internal count to three. If she could retain her current premises, that was definitely the best option, which meant she needed to correct Tobias's false assumption.

She pinned Phillips with a cool glance. "Have you ever seen me before?"

He froze, as if he was under cross-examination. "Uh, not that I can remember."

"That's right, because we have never met. And why would we? You were my aunt's lawyer dealing with her private, personal affairs. Things that have nothing at all to do with me."

Tobias's brows jerked together. "The fact that you didn't meet with Phillips doesn't prove a thing."

Allegra transferred her gaze to Tobias. "You think I took advantage of Esmae while she was on her sickbed and influenced her to change her will. But, if that was the case, why didn't I ask for more, and outright? Like the house and the diamonds, for example? Very expensive assets that she left to you.

"And, before you ask, no, I don't want the house, and I definitely don't want the diamonds—I'm quite capable of getting my own—and I don't need to prove anything about the will. Maybe you should start remembering that I've lived in Miami for just over two years. During that time we've been in the same room, maybe, five times total. Two of those occasions have happened within the space of the last few days—at Esmae's funeral and now. If that's your idea of pursuit, then your love life must have flatlined."

She shoved her copy of the will into her handbag.

Maybe she should have ignored what Tobias had said, but his statement that she was pursuing him had cut too close to the bone because she *had* pursued him, past tense, and been rejected.

On top of that, this whole situation, of being in a room with men who seemed to view her as a woman prepared to use her sex to get what she wanted, was an unpleasant reminder of what she had gone through in San Francisco.

She started for the door, but Tobias reached it first and held it open.

The gesture reminded her that, even online, Tobias had a reputation for being honorable to a fault, and a gentleman. Not that she had experienced that side of his personality.

She sent him a fiery glance and tried not to notice the mouthwatering cut of his cheekbones, or the intriguing hollows beneath, the scar that ran across the bridge of his nose, as if he'd been caught in a bar room brawl or, more likely, been involved in some form of hand-to-hand combat. Unbidden, her stomach tightened at the thought of Tobias in warrior-mode. On the heels of that, a vivid memory of lying in bed with him, their limbs entangled, sent heat flashing through her. Then, she pulled herself up and she was *back*. "You're pointing the finger at me, but maybe *you* were the one who influenced Esmae?"

"Okay, I'll bite," he said mildly. "Why would I want to have you living in my house for a month?"

"Because you're secretly in love with me, can't resist me and, last I heard, it's the only way you'll get a date!"

Stepping through the door, she closed it in his face.

Tobias stared at the smooth mahogany of the door, his attention riveted.

He had tried not to notice the faint sprinkling of freckles across Allegra's nose that reminded him of the windblown young woman who used to hang out at the beach, and the warm flush that had extended across her cheekbones as she'd stared at the scar on his nose.

Or his sudden conviction that Allegra still wanted him.

The knowledge tightened every muscle in Tobias's body, which did not please him one little bit, because Allegra wanting him was the one reason that made sense of Esmae's crazy, manipulative will.

The crack about his difficulty getting a date made him frown. The past couple of years, up until his uncle had retired as the CEO of Hunt Security, he'd been focused on learning the financial side of business. He had spent six months with Gabriel Messena and *had* dated the Messena twins, as it had turned out, on a strictly friend-zone basis.

He had been aware of social media comments around the fact that both Sophie and Francesca Messena had ended up with other guys. But the plain fact was, that as gorgeous as Sophie and Francesca were, they had felt more like sisters than girlfriends.

Now, suddenly, the fact that Allegra had been his last serious date in more than two years struck him forcibly.

Up until that point, he hadn't thought about the lack in his love life, but now his reaction to Allegra, *and hers to him*, was pressing alarm bells.

It was a fact that the reason he had dated Francesca Messena, before and after he had slept with Allegra, was that he had wanted to, once and for all, nix the attraction he felt for Allegra. *And close the door on the "almost" relationship that had caused Lindsay so much pain.*

Unfortunately, the tactic hadn't worked. Dating Francesca hadn't made him stop wanting Allegra.

All she had to do was walk into a room and he reacted—

Phillips, who at some point had gotten to his feet, was also staring at the door. "You going to be all right for the next month? She's, uh…fiery."

"I'll survive."

Even though she'd gone, Allegra's light, flowery perfume seemed to float in the air. Normally, details like the perfumes that women wore went straight over his head, but with Allegra he had trouble forgetting the details. Like the freckles, and the fact that she was wearing the exact same fragrance she had worn when they had made love.

It was a salient reminder that, two years ago, despite all of the reasons he should have left Allegra alone, he *hadn't* been able to resist her. He had abandoned his usual cool reason and had allowed himself to sink into the kind of whirlpool of passion from which it had been difficult to extract himself.

It had taken a bitter phone call from Lindsay, to make him do what he should have done all along, and run a basic online check of Allegra. When he had done so, he had discovered that she had recently been involved in romantic liaisons with at least two West Coast millionaires. The guilt Tobias had felt aside, he had concluded that the one night he and Allegra had shared, as intense as it had been, had been nothing more than another casual liaison.

Plan to have Allegra live with him for a month?

It hadn't been his idea. Maybe Esmae had inserted the clause for the hell of it, to make his life difficult one last time? But, whether Allegra had had a hand in the will or not, the very fact that Esmae, who had doted on her niece, had inserted those clauses, implied that she had done so because she knew Allegra wanted him.

Tobias's pulse rate lifted at the thought.

And there was his problem, he thought grimly. For reasons he couldn't fathom, he still wanted Allegra. There was no logic to it, just a knee-jerk desire that had stayed with him for six years. A desire he had doggedly ignored in the hope it would peter out.

Unfortunately, ignoring what he could only term a fatal attraction hadn't worked.

As he stepped out of Phillips's office, with JT hard on his heels, it occurred to him that maybe it was time to try the tactic he should have used all along.

Let the attraction play out over the next month and die a natural death, like every other attraction to date.

After all, living with Allegra for a month according to the terms of Esmae's will didn't mean anything more than just that. They were sharing a house. If they shared a bed that hardly constituted a relationship, or the marriage for which Esmae was clearly angling.

His whole body tightened at the thought of Allegra back in his bed.

Just one month, and then it would be over.

He didn't know why he hadn't thought of that solution before. Maybe if he had, he would already be free of the inconvenient attraction that to date had nixed every relationship he had attempted to form in the past six years.

He caught sight of Allegra at the end of the corridor as she waited for the elevator to empty. She glanced his way, as if she had sensed him behind her, her gaze clashing with his.

JT, who was in the process of checking his phone, lifted his head. "Maybe she'll hold the elevator for us."

And hell might freeze over.

Given the way Allegra had cut in front of him to take the parking space that morning, then closed Phillips's door in his face, it was a given that she would shut them out.

His jaw compressed as the steel doors glided closed, but at the same time, he felt a fierce jolt of satisfaction, because Allegra hadn't just shut him out; she had also shut out JT. Clearly they weren't as close as JT thought.

Tobias hit the call button on the only other elevator. As he checked the numbers flashing over the door, it occurred to him that the eye contact with Allegra as the elevator doors had closed was an almost-exact replay of what had happened down in the parking garage. That confirmed that she had known he had tailed her into the parking garage and then had deliberately cut him off.

Perversely, the fact that she was boldly crossing swords with him in a way no other woman had ever done, ignited something primitive in him; the urge to answer the challenge when, if he was smart, he would just wait out the month and let her go.

But, even as he formed the thought, he knew he wouldn't do it.

Despite what Allegra had said, he wasn't convinced that she hadn't had a hand in Esmae's will, but the fact that she wanted him seemed to override even that consideration.

The thought of her lying naked in his arms once again made every muscle in his body tighten.

Suddenly, the next month didn't seem like such a prison sentence.

Four

Allegra watched with satisfaction as the floor numbers flashed while the elevator descended to the underground garage.

The moment she had seen Tobias exiting Phillips's office with JT directly behind him replayed. Adrenaline had pumped as Tobias's eyes had locked with hers. That in itself had been annoying, but not as annoying as the fact that, evidently, he had expected her to *want* to stay eye-locked with him as he had strode toward her.

As if she was some kind of Barbie doll robot just waiting for him to activate her.

No way was Tobias even remotely that important in her life, so she had stepped into the elevator and hit the close door button. It was a small act of revenge but, after the scene in Phillips's office, there was no way either Tobias or JT should expect to share an elevator with her. Happily, she had timed things nicely, so they hadn't even been close when the doors had snapped shut, sealing her into blissful isolation.

On the way down, she checked her hair and makeup in the mirror. Despite all of the turmoil, she looked almost as smooth and composed as she had when she'd left home. That was thanks to the beauty pageant circuit, which had taught her that, no matter what went on in the dressing rooms, you stepped out on the stage with a smile on your face.

Humming beneath her breath, she found her ear pods, put them in her ears and dialed up some soothing music on her phone, then spent the remaining seconds watching the numbers flash over the door until the elevator came to a halt. A few seconds later, an elderly man sporting a cane, who was cute and kind of reminded her of her granddad, trundled in the door and peered at the numbers, as if he was confused.

A quick conversation, and the press of a button, and she had him sorted out. As the elevator lurched into action again, she realized she was still breathing a little too fast. Technically, she was hyperventilating, which was not good. She needed to breathe deep and slow.

The elevator stopped for the old guy to get off, and while she waited for the doors to close and start speeding down again, she checked the heart rate app on her watch. The last thing she needed was another

SVT event, because those attacks, as easy as they were to fix, were *scary*.

Just over two years ago, when she had ended up in the ER, following the "interview" with the partners at Burns-Stein Halliday, she had listened to her doctor's advice then consulted the oracle—that was her mom—before deciding to make some changes in her life.

Both of her parents had wanted to bring charges against Burns-Stein Halliday for sexual harassment in the workplace. Her mom had even threatened to "go over there," and that was some scary stuff. But Allegra definitely hadn't wanted the stress of a court case, which could have landed her back in the hospital, or worse.

The last thing she had wanted was to *die* or end up in some clinic somewhere, making baskets, all because BSH was a horrible employer. The way she saw it, she owed it to her parents, and the world at large (not BSH, she didn't owe them anything) to stay happy, and stay alive.

Once she had made the decision not to sue BSH, it had been an easy step to embrace a career that was founded on the two things she knew she was good at: money *and* beauty.

A few weeks holiday with Esmae in her private beach mansion had given her the inspiration she needed to start up her own retreat spa.

Esmae, who had been something of a risk-taker and adventurer in her younger days, had offered to back her, mostly because she was tired of being treated like she was old and washed-up, and so Madison Spas had been born. The name *Madison* had seemed appropriate, because that was a second name they both shared.

The spa had been up and running for almost two years now, and, in that time, she had expanded to offer a number of beauty and pampering treatments. Lately, it had become something of a destination for burned-out celebrities needing to recharge, hence her need to open a second retreat, this one in a more remote location.

She had already earmarked a possible property. Once she got past the hurdle of the next month, she would be able to have a conversation with her bank manager and arrange the finances she needed to expand.

In the meantime, Esmae's will had literally locked her and Tobias together for the next month.

Logically, she had known that the resort would go to Tobias, because the place had been built on Hunt money. She just hadn't thought he would turn up in person to take over as manager.

Now, not only was her life totally ruined for the next four weeks because she had to share a house with Tobias, but Esmae had also managed to throw them together in their working lives!

The terms of the will had left zero doubt that Esmae was attempting to matchmake from beyond the grave. And, to make matters worse, Allegra was pretty much sure it *was* all her fault, because, somehow, Esmae had gotten the mistaken idea that she still wanted Tobias.

The elevator doors opened to the darkened underground garage.

Strolling at a moderate pace, because her shoes were too high for anything more than a sedate saunter, and still listening to the soothing music, she made a beeline for her car. The sound of the second set of elevator doors opening behind her, which she could still hear quite well because the ear pods were the expensive kind that let you hear everything else as well as the music, sent tension humming through her. Despite the temptation to speed up her pace, she kept her gait smooth and even. So what if it was Tobias? He didn't scare her—

"Allegra."

Despite her confidence, the deep, curt tones of his voice made her stomach tighten, but she kept her pace smooth and unaltered. After all, she had *ear pods* in; chances were she hadn't heard him.

The sound of footsteps sent tension humming through her. As tempting as it was to speed up, she kept her languid stroll, but took out her phone for good measure, so Tobias could see she was doubly busy.

The next second her phone rang. It registered an unknown caller, but she knew exactly who it was.

She hit the accept call button. "How did you get my number?"

Tobias's deep, curt voice filled her ear. "You gave it to me two years ago."

Wrong answer. "I took it back."

"Then I guess I must have forgotten to delete it."

"What do you want?"

"Turn around and find out."

Stabbing the disconnect button, she threw a seemingly confused look over her shoulder, as if she hadn't understood that Tobias, accompanied by JT, had been behind her all along. "Oh, it's…you."

She made a show of removing the ear pods. "Sorry. Were you trying to talk to me?"

Amusement surfaced in Tobias's gaze. He dangled a key. "You're going to need this."

Allegra instantly recognized the pretty beaded key chain, because it was the same one she had used when she had lived with Esmae, before she'd found her apartment.

Taking care not to brush his fingers with hers, she took the key but, as she did so, emotion welled up. It was still so hard to believe that Esmae, who had made her feel so at home in Miami, was gone.

She met Tobias's gaze squarely, suddenly glad she had decided to wear such ridiculously high heels, otherwise she would have had to tip her head back to do so. "Thanks. Although, for the record, I do not want to live with you—"

"We won't be *living* together."

Her gaze narrowed. The knowledge that, despite everything she had said in Phillips's office, Tobias really did think she was after him, and was scheming to trap him, settled in.

She had always wondered where the impulse to hit someone came from. Now, she knew.

JT offered Allegra a good-ole-boy smile. "Honey, I think Tobias knows you don't want to *live* with him. I mean, you've already said why, chapter and verse—"

"Don't call me Honey." The words flowed out, cool and crisp, cutting JT off, so that he stared at her, surprised.

Allegra hadn't meant to offend JT, who was an occasional client, especially not when he had been defending her. But he hadn't exactly been her friend in Phillips's office, and, since the horrible events of San Francisco, she'd developed a zero tolerance for that kind of casual intimacy.

Tobias slanted JT a pointed look. "You should stay out of this."

JT backed off a step, his expression wary. "No problem. Not my fight—"

"That's right."

"Okay. Well…" JT shrugged. "I'm on my way back to the office."

JT's footsteps echoed through the garage as he headed for his car, but, now that they were alone, the tension between her and Tobias was suddenly thick enough to cut.

Tobias frowned. "You've done something to your nose."

Taken off guard by the change in tack, Allegra automatically touched the side of the bridge of her nose, which had once been marred by a small bump.

The bump had only been discernible from certain angles, but after being ditched by Tobias, the imperfection, which came from the Toussaint side of the family, had seemed to glare back at her every time she looked in the mirror. "I had surgery to fix it. It wasn't a big deal."

Tobias gaze shifted. "And you've changed your hair."

She blinked, for long moments transfixed by the color of his irises, which seemed softer and darker than she remembered, fringed as they were by inky lashes. She dragged her gaze free, breaking the moment. The problem was, she didn't know whether to feel pleasure that Tobias had noticed the surgery or her hair color, or irritated for the same reason.

She shoved the house key in a zip pocket in her handbag, along with her ear pods, while she tried to figure out why on earth he was almost complimenting her. When she couldn't, because there was no way he could be trying to sweet-talk her into a date, she decided to keep things neutral and treat him with politeness, like she would a client. Who knows? The politeness might even rub off on him. "Thank you for noticing. I haven't changed anything—that's my natural color. I *used* to color it with blond streaks, but since the spa provides natural therapies and detoxification regimes, it wouldn't look good if I showed up for work as a bottle blond."

But, underneath all of her annoyance with Tobias, she couldn't quite suppress the warm, fuzzy feeling of pleasure that he had noticed the changes she'd made.

Then a horror-filled thought nixed the pleasure. Now that she *had* to share a house with Tobias, could he possibly be thinking that she would be open to sharing his bed, on a strictly casual basis, of course?

Suddenly, the month with Tobias seemed even more fraught. Two years ago, she had fallen for him and thrown caution to the winds. If he seriously set out to seduce her now, would she be strong enough to resist him?

Out of the blue, a solution settled into place. It was the perfect answer to a situation that seemed to be getting way out of hand.

Digging her car keys out of her bag, and sticking with the business owner/client synergy, she plastered a neutral smile on her face. "As I was saying…one of the reasons I don't want to share a house with you is that…" She drew a deep breath and crossed the fingers of one hand behind her back. "*My fiancé* won't exactly be happy if I move in with you."

The slam of JT's car door and the cough of his car starting echoed through the cavernous space.

For a weird moment, Tobias's face looked like thunder, and she actually got the impression that he was going to argue with her, then his expression cleared.

He glanced at her left hand, which was, of course, bare. "I didn't know you were engaged."

Allegra still had the fingers of her right hand crossed behind her back. She had lied, and she *never* lied. But, even though she hated having to do that, she had to continue with the charade now. "Why would you? We're not exactly friends."

JT's car cruised toward them, heading for the exit. Tobias stepped out of the lane, closer to the vehicle they were both standing next to, and lifted a hand as JT went past. When he produced a key, a small shock went through Allegra, because she realized they were standing right next to his black truck. Somehow, he had managed to find a space just two down from where her convertible was parked.

The lights of the truck flashed as he unlocked it. "Strange that Esmae didn't mention your engagement."

Allegra kept her cool, professional smile on her face, but her mind was going a million miles an hour. She was going to have to find an actual fiancé now, which was problematic, since lately she'd been so busy with plans for the new retreat property she had even stopped dating. She didn't know if she even knew anyone who could fill the role.

"Esmae didn't know," she said smoothly, "because it's…only just happened."

Tobias's gaze seemed to laser through her. "Interesting. So when, exactly, did you get engaged? At the funeral?"

Allegra suppressed the urge to snap that it was none of his business. But now was not the time to lose her cool. Besides, she was struck by how irritable Tobias was, even more annoyed than he'd been in Phillips's office. He had been short with JT, now he was needling her, as if her engagement had somehow added to his aggravation, which didn't make sense.

He should be dancing in the street. Unless it mattered to him that she was engaged.

Unless he was jealous.

She instantly dismissed the notion. There was just no way, because, if Tobias was jealous, that meant he cared for her, and pigs would fly before that happened.

Thinking quickly, she tried to come up with a believable date for getting engaged. "We got engaged—the day before the funeral."

"You worked the day before."

Her gaze narrowed at his knowledge of her schedule and the way he kept questioning her, as if he didn't believe she could be engaged. With an effort of will, she kept her smile in place. "I'm a woman," she said flatly, "I multitask. Besides, I don't work twenty-four hours of every day. When the spa closes I have…a life."

His gaze pinned her in place, before dropping to her mouth, sending tension zinging through her. She was even getting a weird feeling low in her belly, as if she were actually just the tiniest bit turned on, which *couldn't* be.

"So, who's the lucky guy?"

Her phone rang. Talk about saved by the bell, because her mind was utterly blank on the subject of who could possibly be her fiancé.

She extracted her cell phone out of her handbag just as the call, which was from one of her suppliers, was transferred to voice mail. But the fact that it was a work call provided her with the inspiration she needed.

She had recently employed a gym instructor and personal trainer, Mike. A part-time model and actor waiting for his big break, Mike was tall, muscled and blond, and looked like a Norse hero. He wasn't exactly the brightest person on her team and he had an offbeat humor and a narcissistic streak that could be challenging, but he *was* gorgeous. He was also cash-strapped and had recently asked her for more hours.

That, along with his acting training, made him perfect for the part.

Allegra tried to look as if she'd just remembered Tobias's question. "His name's Mike, uh—" she was so used to calling Mike by just his first name that, for a second she had trouble remembering his surname "—*Callaghan.* You'll meet him soon enough. Although," she said smoothly, "I shouldn't have said anything, since we haven't announced it yet."

She checked her watch, as if she was suddenly in a hurry, which she was, now that she had an engagement to organize. "How soon do I have to move into the house?" She could not quite bring herself to say *your house.*

Tobias crossed his arms over his chest. "Today, if you want."

"Great. The sooner it's over the better, because I'd like to have some privacy to be with my fiancé."

Something heated flashed in his gaze. "I'll be moving in this afternoon, as well."

She busied herself sliding her phone back in her bag. "Naturally, Mike will be helping me. Maybe he can also give you a hand if you need it? He's really strong."

A glint of humor surfaced. "I don't need a hand. It's not as if I'm staying out there more than the month."

She offered him the kind of distant smile she used to end conversations with people she had not wanted to talk to in the first place. "Just one month and we'll both have what we're entitled to, and then we can go our separate ways."

The amusement disappeared from Tobias's gaze. "Spoken like a true Mallory."

The way he said it stung. Of course, he had known that Esmae had backed her financially, but her assistance hadn't been necessary. "For your information, I tried to buy back those shares from Esmae four months ago."

"I'd believe that if she hadn't written her new will around the time she went into partnership with you."

"So you think I made the offer already knowing Esmae was giving me the shares?"

Something snapped. Before she could stop herself, she stepped close enough to Tobias that she could feel the heat blasting off his body and smell the clean scents of soap and whatever that cologne was, and jabbed a finger at his chest. "You make it sound like I'm dishonest, which is entirely your business, but it's a fact that I'm entirely capable of raising my own finances, which is what I would have done if

Esmae hadn't been so set on wanting an interest in Madison Spas."

She glared at him. "And, for the record…neither is my family, either past or present, dishonest. The Mallorys have had their share of luck, good and bad, just like the Hunts. And, before you say it, I know the story about Jebediah and Alexandra and, quite frankly, I'm over it. If you ask me, the reason Jebediah went so sour on Alexandra wasn't because he ended up with a piece of land that didn't have an oil well on it. It was because Alexandra rejected him and found *someone else*. Someone who was probably a whole lot nicer."

She could say more. The way Tobias's family told the story about Esmae's marriage to Michael Hunt was equally objectionable. As far as Allegra was concerned, the implication that Esmae had been a scheming gold digger was utterly ridiculous, because Esmae Mallory had been gorgeous enough to marry anyone she chose. What's more, Allegra had the pictures to prove it. "And let's talk about the elephant in the room. The Hunt family is hugely successful and rich. You could buy and sell the oil well Alexandra ended up with, *out of sheer good luck*, a million times over and still have change. So why don't we just park the whole story and move on!"

"This is why," he muttered.

Tobias's hands landed at her waist, his head dipped and his mouth landed on hers. As kisses went it was light, almost tentative, or would have been if she hadn't swayed off-balance and gripped the lapels of his jacket.

His arms came around her waist, and all the breath went from her lungs as he pressed her close enough that she could feel the hard wall of his chest, the pound of his heart and the riveting fact that he was aroused.

At that point, a hot little pang shot through her, and her knees went as limp as noodles. Dimly, she was aware that the strap of her handbag had slipped off her shoulder and the bag was now on the concrete floor. But she couldn't worry about that, it was all she could do to hold on to Tobias's shoulders, as she angled her jaw to deepen the kiss.

Tobias muttered something else under his breath, that sounded suspiciously like a swear word. His hands cupped her bottom and she was hauled even closer, then upward, so that her feet were left dangling. She wound her arms around his neck and hung on. A split second later, she felt the cold solidity of metal behind her, as he settled her against the cold steel of the truck.

The sound of the elevator doors opening made her stiffen. Heat flushed through her as she realized what she was doing, what she had allowed. They were practically making love against the side of Tobias's truck. Embarrassed at the way she had clung on to him, she wriggled free and smoothed her dress, which had hiked up, back down around her thighs.

Dragging in a breath, she stepped back, then had

to grip the edge of the truck because her legs still felt unsteady. "That shouldn't have happened."

Tobias straightened his tie, which she must have dragged loose. "Because you're engaged?"

Allegra's cheeks warmed. She had almost forgotten that part. *"Yes."*

A middle-aged man with a briefcase walked past them, an interested gleam in his gaze.

It was at that point she realized that a button on her bodice had popped open, exposing more than just a hint of cleavage. Fumbling in her haste, she rebuttoned the bodice, then bent down and retrieved her gorgeous Messena handbag, which was now covered in dust smudges. Tobias retrieved a lipstick and a vial of perfume that had rolled beneath the truck. Feeling flustered because she had kissed Tobias back, she snatched back her personal items.

She rummaged in her bag and found her car keys. "That can't happen again."

"You're the boss," he growled.

She sent him a fiery glance. She wasn't sensing any regret, in fact, just the opposite. There was still a heated gleam, right alongside the bad-tempered attitude, and then she finally figured it out. There was no way a guy could fake arousal, and she had been plastered against Tobias, so he hadn't been able to hide the fact that he was aroused, either.

Tobias wanted her.

The problem was, he wanted her *against his will*, which was more than a little insulting, and brought back the hurt and humiliation of Tobias ditching her two years ago.

As far as she was concerned, in behaving that way, Tobias had committed *the* cardinal sin: he had trivialized her.

She didn't need a crystal ball to know that he had bought into the fake news propagated by Halliday and Fischer on their toxic social media pages.

He was probably, even now, making some kind of superficial value judgment about her but, thankfully, because she had such a kickass attitude, what Tobias thought would absolutely *not* affect her. One of the reasons she hadn't dated a lot in high school or college, and had made the mistake of going to an executive dating site, was that very reason. Usually, she could spot the kind of guy who was going to make shallow assumptions about her a mile off. The second she figured it out, she walked because, newsflash, she was just not interested in spending time with a guy who only saw her as a cliché.

Turning on her heel, she stalked toward her car. She needed to think, and fast, because now she had to figure a way to get through a whole month with a Tobias who wanted her.

Then she remembered Mike. Duh.

Opening the driver's-side door, she placed her bag on the passenger seat, slid behind the wheel and closed her door with an expensive *thunk*. She was just about to start the car when Tobias walked around the rear, leaned down and placed both hands on her door, preventing her from backing out of the space.

"Just so we make one thing clear. Your *fiancé* can help you move in, but that's where it ends. He can't stay."

Allegra could feel the color rising in her cheeks, not just at Tobias's dictatorial manner, but at the way he had said *fiancé*, as if he didn't really believe she had one.

She pressed the starter button of the car. The engine purred to life, which was a handy way of letting Tobias know that the conversation was over.

The fact that he clearly didn't believe her, besides being insulting, made her all the more determined to employ Mike for the role. She didn't know what she would have to pay him, but if she had to empty her personal bank account, she would do it.

It was bad enough that she was going to have to live in Tobias's house for a month, but his high-handed manner in laying down the rules about her seeing her fiancé—even though Mike wouldn't really be her fiancé—burned.

By the time she moved into Esmae's—*Tobias's*—house, her fake engagement had to be fully operational.

Tobias released her door, but she wasn't quite ready to leave.

Tilting her head back, she gazed at Tobias from beneath her lashes. She had practiced that look in the mirror and while doing selfies until she had perfected it, and she knew it was crazy hot.

Maybe goading Tobias at this point wasn't the smartest choice, but the last time she had taken orders she had been three. And, even at that age, she had known that last order had been reasonable, because if she had eaten all of the cookies in the cookie jar she *would* have been sick. "Are you trying to tell me that I can't have sex with my fiancé?"

Something dangerous flashed in Tobias's eyes, as if she had finally pushed him over the edge of a precipice she hadn't known was there. Out of nowhere a hot thrill shot down her spine.

"Not in my house," he said softly.

Their gazes locked with a laser intensity she was having difficulty breaking, probably because Tobias's eyes had a magnetic, mesmerizing quality, which, somehow, made all brain function stop.

Approximately ninety seconds ago, she had figured out that Tobias wanted her. Now, she had another vital piece of information.

He didn't want Mike to have her.

Which meant he *was* jealous.

Another hot thrill, this one going all the way to you-know-where, practically welded her in place. "Oh good," she said, injecting a brisk, businesslike note into her voice. "For a moment there I thought you were saying I couldn't have sex with my fiancé at all!"

Before she could become completely paralyzed from the hypnotic effect of Tobias's gaze, *and agree to sleep with him again*, she put the car into Reverse, backed out of the space, then shot toward the exit. She was almost at the turn into the exit ramp when another vehicle reversed into the lane.

Braking, she waited, fingers tense on the wheel. A faint tingling at the back of her neck had her checking the rearview mirror. Tobias's truck glided in behind her, once again dwarfing her small car.

She should have waited for him to leave first, because now she was stuck with Tobias behind her until she could get out of the building. Like the drive in, his big black truck was making her feel distinctly herded, which was a feeling she had never experienced until Tobias.

In the past, there had been occasions when guys had deliberately followed her to get her attention, but the most she had felt was irritation. She had literally batted them off like flies.

The SUV in front finally achieved some forward motion. Relief washed through Allegra when she finally turned onto the city street. The little café where she was buying lunch was on the coast, and Tobias's office was in the center of town, so he would have to turn in the opposite direction.

When he did so, she relaxed a fraction more, but the feminine tension that had spun out of control when they had kissed was still keeping her on edge.

Annoyed at the way she was still reacting, she shifted in her seat and rolled her shoulders to try and relax her muscles, but vivid flashes of what it had felt like to kiss Tobias and be pressed close against him, kept ratcheting up the tension.

She braked for a light, then checked her mirror. Another hot pang shot through her when she spied the rear of Tobias's truck, even though it was at a distance.

A car horn blared. Depressing the accelerator, she drove through the intersection and, just in time, remembered to take the lane that led toward the beach.

The problem was that, for reasons she couldn't fathom, she was turned on. The feelings had sneaked up on her, but this time she would not be caught off guard.

After months of therapy and graduating from a series of online relationship empowerment classes for women, she was now equipped with a degree of emotional intelligence she hadn't possessed when she had made the mistake of sleeping with Tobias.

Despite still wanting him, she now knew exactly what she was coping with: a fatal attraction. What's more, she had the tools in place to resist Tobias.

She was forewarned, forearmed and she was "engaged."

The fact that Tobias had kissed her after he had learned she had a fiancé made her frown. The only reason that explained his total lack of respect for the fact that she was pledged to another man, was that he hadn't believed in the engagement.

Just like he hadn't believed her when she had told him she wasn't trying to trap him into marriage.

That meant that, despite her efforts to prove that she didn't want him, he was still convinced that she did.

That meant she *definitely* had to have the engagement visible, and in Tobias's face, by this afternoon.

Five

Tobias strode into his downtown office and lifted a hand to Jean, his indomitable, indispensible PA, before stepping into the inner sanctum of his office.

Tossing his briefcase on a leather chair, he walked to the huge wall of glass that offered spectacular views out over the cityscape, with glimpses of Miami Beach, and out to sea. Although, for long seconds the view didn't register at all, because he was back in the darkened underground garage, with Allegra Mallory winding her arms around his neck and stretching her taut, curvy body against him as the first kiss had turned into a second and then a third.

He had come close to losing it. He knew it, and so did Allegra. And all because she had dropped her bombshell about having a fiancé, a piece of information that should have filled him with relief but which, instead, had had the opposite effect.

The fiery tension that had burned through him when she'd announced her engagement was still humming through him.

Allegra, engaged?

Not if he had his way.

Allegra Mallory was his.

The thought settled in with a curious inevitability. Why, exactly, he wanted Allegra was unclear. He knew plenty of beautiful, intelligent, charming women. Over the past two years he had done his share of dating, specifically to cure himself of whatever it was he felt for Allegra.

Six years ago, it had hit him like a bolt from the blue. Two years ago, it had resulted in his breaking up with his fiancée, Lindsay. The power of the attraction had been strong enough that, even though he was certain the stress of the break-up had contributed to Lindsay's miscarriage, he hadn't been able to forget Allegra.

Every time she walked into a room, despite the guilt that still gnawed at him, every muscle in his body tightened—

His door popped open. JT walked in, with a pizza box and a box of doughnuts balanced on one hand, a bottle of soda in the other. He lifted a brow. "Peace offering? Didn't realize I was…you know, stepping on your toes."

Tobias met the other man's gaze for a long moment. He had been short and to-the-point, but he didn't regret it. JT had needed to know that Allegra was off-limits. "If it helps," he said grimly, "*I* didn't know it until right then." He checked out the pizza and the doughnuts and shook his head. "Lunch?"

"More like two glorious works of art." JT put the pizza, the doughnuts, the soda and a small stack of napkins on his coffee table. He helped himself to a seat and opened the lid on the pizza box. "Double cheese with fennel sausage *and* prosciutto. And the doughnuts are salted caramel with vanilla cream."

"You are going to die."

"And go to heaven." JT loaded a slice of pizza onto a napkin. "Now that you've apologized, you can have some pizza."

Pizza wasn't exactly his lunch of choice, but since he hadn't actually eaten today, apart from the coffee on the red-eye flight from New York, Tobias accepted a slice. But he was still too wound up to sit.

When he'd finished, JT passed him a napkin. "So…you and Allegra. I guess I should have remembered that you, uh, slept with her."

Tobias's brows jerked together. "How did you know about that?"

"I was at Esmae's ninetieth birthday party. I just happened to see you two down on the beach."

"That was two years ago. Times have changed." Tobias wiped his fingers with the napkin, then tossed it into the trash. "Apparently, she's engaged."

JT stopped dead, a slice of pizza part way to his mouth. "You're kidding. That's the first I've heard of it and, in this town, I hear *a lot* of stuff." He set the pizza down, underlining the gravity of the moment. "I mean, with Allegra looking the way she does, she's not exactly invisible. There are a lot of guys who would *happily*—"

"Stop right there, JT."

"Yeah. Uh—sorry." JT wiped his fingers with a napkin and tried for a rueful smile. "Well, I guess if she's engaged that means she's probably not dying to get her hot hands on you, after all. Although…" He closed the lid of the empty pizza box and zeroed in on the doughnuts. "What if the engagement's just a ploy, and she's trying to make herself more attractive? You know, make out she's—" he sketched quotation marks in the air ""—unavailable.""

"Allegra's been in Miami, living less than a mile from my apartment, and successfully avoiding me for two years, so the availability theory doesn't exactly hold up."

Shrugging, JT selected a doughnut. "So the engagement's real. That sucks. Wonder who the lucky guy is?"

Tobias found himself controlling his temper with difficulty. "Someone called Mike Callaghan."

"Thor? No way." He took a bite of the doughnut and chewed reflectively. "Not that he's actually the Norse god of thunder—he's the personal trainer at the spa. Julia did a couple of sessions with him, just before we broke up. At least that explains it. He's some serious eye candy, *and* they work together."

Tobias's jaw tightened. Up until that moment, Callaghan hadn't seemed entirely real. In fact, Tobias had gotten the distinct impression that Allegra had pulled a name out of a hat.

And, as it happened, Tobias had made it his business to know whom Allegra was seeing. The surveillance hadn't been exhaustive. Mostly, he had checked out her social media sites when he had a spare hour in the evenings. The overriding impression was that she had only dated on a casual level. Two, maybe three dates, was all she ever committed to with one guy, and he couldn't recall ever seeing Callaghan's name.

But the fact that she worked with the guy changed things, because that meant she saw him on a daily basis. Suddenly, the thought of Allegra in bed with Callaghan didn't seem like such a stretch.

The tension that was coursing through him was oddly clarifying. He realized he was grimly, burningly jealous, but at least the feelings clarified what he had felt in Phillips's office and in the parking garage.

He wanted Allegra.

He didn't know for how long he would want her. Despite the complication of the will, and the mistakes of the past that still haunted him, his feelings for Allegra were, as they had been all along, curiously black-and-white.

He just wanted her, period, and he knew that, even though wild horses wouldn't drag it from her, that she wanted him, too.

He was also aware that, with Callaghan now firmly in the picture, if he didn't claim Allegra now, *today*, he could lose her completely.

* * *

When JT finally left, Tobias looked at the carnage of his office, the overflowing trash can, the soda spills and the clouds of powdered sugar that seemed to have settled on every available surface. Not for the first time, he thought about what life would be like without JT, then, almost immediately, dismissed the thought.

He had known JT most of his life. They'd gone to school and through BUDs together. As annoying as he could be, JT was the closest thing to a brother that Tobias had.

On impulse, he dialed his PA's number. Even though he'd eaten a slice of pizza, he still felt hungry and, since he was moving into Esmae's house straight after the Ocean Beach meeting, it made sense to get something now.

There was a café on the ground floor of the building that Jean liked. If he wanted to eat in, she usually got them to send up sandwiches and salads.

When he gave her his request, she was silent for a beat. "You don't want beef?"

"I'd like to try something—different."

"How different?" she said cautiously. "There are at least a dozen vegetarian dishes."

Tobias frowned. "What do you like?"

"Me? I usually have the vegetarian stack, or sometimes lentil patties or a wild rice salad." She paused. "Maybe you should have fish. They have a very nice salmon quiche—"

"I'll try all the things you listed."

An hour later, Tobias finished sampling the variety of vegetarian dishes the café had delivered. They weren't bad; there was nothing he disliked. The problem was he was still hungry. The only thing he'd really enjoyed had been the coffee. Whether it was psychological or not, the food he'd eaten had failed to satisfy.

Like his love life.

He checked his watch. In less than an hour, he had to drive to the Ocean Beach Resort for his meeting with the manager, Marc Porter. Over the next month, like it or not, he was going to have to come to grips with running a luxury resort, something he knew very little about.

The only positive was that Esmae had had a talent for surrounding herself with young, highly qualified staff, and the present manager was a case in point. The biggest issue was Allegra's spa. He didn't have access to those figures. All he had was a copy of the lease agreement with the resort, which expired in two month's time.

It made sense not to renew the lease. The way he saw it, Esmae's passing meant he could once-for-all sever his connection to Allegra, *and remove the temptation she posed from his life.* But the fact that he wanted Allegra back in his bed had changed things somewhat.

Madison Spas still had to go. Allegra wouldn't be happy, but he would make it up to her. He could even soften the blow by finding her alternative premises before he terminated the lease.

Whatever the issues were, they were solvable. But *after* he had gotten her back in his bed.

Allegra parked her car in its space at the Ocean Beach Resort and strolled into the premises that housed her spa. Not for the first time, her heart swelled with pride at what she'd achieved.

Ocean Beach was a luxurious resort, which catered to the affluent and those wanting a beach holiday. Her spa offered the beach vibe as well, but she had gone out of her way to create secluded gardens and quiet spaces where solitude could be enjoyed. Most of her clientele stayed at the resort proper, and came for various treatments or half or full-day packages, but she did have secluded cabins for clients who wanted the privacy and quietness of a retreat stay.

Once she reached her office, she checked the schedule of activities, specifically to find out where she might find Mike. Gym classes were finished for the day, but he did have one client booked for a personal training session, which was set to finish any minute.

She walked through to the gym, which was airy and light and outfitted with the latest state-of-the-art equipment, as well as a mirrored wall for dance classes. Mike was presently leaning against a weight-lifting frame, stopwatch in his hand, while his client, a plump, Asian executive-type Allegra recognized as one of their most faithful regulars, attempted to do lunges.

Mike directed an amiable grin in her direction, hit

the stopwatch app on his smartwatch and clapped his client on the shoulder. "Better live to fight another day, eh James? Hit the showers, and I'll see you at six in the morning for that run on the beach."

James was aghast. "Six?"

Mike slung a towel around his neck and picked up his gym bag. "Unless you want to go earlier?"

"Arrgh… Six is fine."

Allegra waited until the executive staggered through the door that led to the showers before opening what was going to be an awkward conversation.

Mike, who refused to wear glasses while he was working, pushed a pair of horn-rimmed glasses onto the bridge of his nose as he ambled toward her. "Hey. What's up, boss?"

Allegra gave him her best professional smile. "Last week you asked me for more hours. At the time, I didn't have any extra work, but something's cropped up."

Mike gave her a distracted grin as he dug in his gym bag. "Sounds like that could be promising for me." He found his phone. "Did you decide to run with my proposal for a cage-fighting class in that bit of jungle down by the beach?"

"Not exactly. Most of our clients come here to wind down, so I can't really see how something like that is going to work." There was no easy way to say it. "The extra hours would be more in the line of *acting* than physical training."

"Acting? Cool." Mike frowned as he flicked through something on his phone. He peered at her over the top of his glasses, which were clearly for distance, not close reading. "How did you know I was looking for an acting gig?"

Allegra frowned. She did not exactly see the fake engagement as a "gig." "You told me. In the interview."

"Phew, that's a relief! Because when I get my big break, I'll be gone." He made a sudden, swooping plane-like movement with his hand, then went back to flicking through texts. "I've been waiting for my agent to contact me about a part in a new daytime soap. Some kind of *Baywatch* meets aliens and zombies thing."

Allegra took a deep breath and determinedly put her irritation to one side. "In the meantime, like I said, I do have an acting job of sorts for you." She mentioned a figure.

Mike looked up from his phone and grinned. "Who do I have to sleep with to get that?"

"You won't be sleeping with anyone," Allegra said frostily. "The job is strictly window dressing." She drew a deep breath, but there was no point in beating around the bush. "I need a fake fiancé for a month."

Mike stared at her as if she'd just grown an extra head. "Why would you want a fake fiancé?"

"It's…complicated."

He frowned, as if he was having trouble getting his head around the concept. "So, you need an *escort*? I mean, I did it for a while, but I hated the hours and the bars. Kind of messed up my fitness routine. Then there was the whole cougar thing…"

Allegra's brows jerked together. "Do I look like a cougar?"

Mike blinked. "No, ma'am. You look like my boss."

"Exactly." Allegra was beginning to think she had made a major mistake in asking Mike. From what she could remember of his curriculum vitae there had been a lot of detail about his personal training, modeling and acting abilities. There had been no mention that he had ever worked as a male escort. "I don't need an escort. I need an *actor.*"

Mike frowned, then nodded, as if he had finally gotten it. "So all I have to do is *pretend* to like you."

"Pretend to be my fiancé," she corrected. Then, because she was beginning to think Mike had gotten his wires crossed over what the job entailed, she clarified, "This does not involve sex in any way, shape or form."

"And you still want to pay all that money?" He grinned, and, for a minute, she thought he was actually going to try and high-five her. "Cool."

When she got home that evening, Allegra changed into a cotton dress that was airy and easy to move in, because she would be doing a lot of lifting, and slipped on a comfortable pair of sneakers. She packed two suitcases with everything she would conceivably need over the next month, then did a tour of the bathroom, gathering up toiletries.

She had made sure to include some evening wear, because she had planned a schedule of dates with

Mike to cement the fact that they were an engaged couple. She had also packed her jewelry case, which was filled with an assortment of significant jewelry she would not feel comfortable with leaving in an empty apartment, as well as some cheap and glitzy pageant bling. If she had forgotten anything, it would be an easy enough matter to call back to her apartment.

She wheeled the suitcases to her front door. Normally, she would have carried them out to her garage and loaded them into her car herself. However, because Mike had agreed to meet her at her apartment, she figured that, as part of his role, he could take care of her baggage.

She did a quick check of the apartment to make sure the windows were locked, then grabbed a shopping tote and emptied perishables from the pantry and the refrigerator. Esmae used to have a couple live in with her, but since she'd been in the hospital, she had switched to having them just call in to look after the grounds and check the house. That being the case, there wasn't likely to be any fresh food at the house. She set the tote next to her suitcases, then checked her watch, noting that Mike was ten minutes late.

Feeling a familiar sense of irritation at Mike's casual attitude toward time, she made a start on loading the bags herself. After all, the important part of Mike helping her move was that he *unloaded* everything and carried it to her rooms while Tobias watched.

Getting the bags into her little convertible was a

mission, courtesy of the fact that it was a two door. With difficulty, she managed to wedge the smaller one in the space behind the front seats and prop the largest bag in the passenger seat. The bag of perishables went on the floor, along with her handbag.

Feeling on edge, she walked back into the house and did a last check that she hadn't forgotten anything, ending up in her cool, stylish bedroom with its white-on-white decor and pretty little terrace. On impulse, she checked her appearance, since the last thing she wanted was to turn up at Tobias's house with smudged makeup or messy hair.

Her mineral-based foundation, which, naturally, was the same brand her spa sold, looked smooth and perfect. Her eye makeup was subtle, but smoky, making her eyes look even darker. On impulse, she rummaged through the drawers, found extra hairpins and fastened the knot in her hair more securely.

When Mike eventually arrived in his beaten-up truck, which sprouted rusted fishing rod holders, it was a good twenty minutes past the time they had agreed, and the sun was sinking low on the horizon. Keeping her irritation in check, because it would have been so much easier to have loaded the bags into his truck than squeeze them into her convertible, Allegra gave him a copy of the schedule of dates she had formulated that afternoon and instructed him to follow her to the mansion.

Twenty minutes later, she drove through the gorgeous wrought iron gates that guarded the driveway to the Spanish-style mansion and pulled up in the circular area of gravel outside the front doors. Her heart thumped against her chest when she saw Tobias's black truck already parked, indicating he was in the process of moving in.

Allegra pushed her door open and climbed out, just as Mike's truck pulled to a halt behind her. Walking around the sleek exterior of her car, she opened the passenger-side door, unfastened the seat belt, then began wrangling the suitcase, until she remembered Mike was supposed to do it.

Feeling exasperated, she abandoned the case. For some reason, Mike was still sitting in his truck. The reason became evident when she discovered that he was intently reading the dating schedule.

She knocked on his window. "You're supposed to be helping me."

He wound down his window and pointed to the first sentence of the schedule. "You want me to do this first scene, right now?"

For a moment, she was actually speechless. "It's not a scene, Mike. It's real life."

"Oh…yeah!" Grinning, Mike climbed out of his truck and folded and jammed the pages of the schedule into the back pocket of his jeans.

Allegra drew a deep breath and attempted to relax. "Don't forget, you're supposed to be pretending to be my fiancé." A little grimly, she noted he had his glasses on, which was not ideal, because he looked far more impressive without them. She was about to tell him to take them off, put them in the truck and leave them there, but then the front door to the mansion popped open.

Tobias strode down the front steps, looking more muscular than she remembered in faded jeans and a T-shirt that molded his broad shoulders. His gaze immediately went to Mike, who was in the process of hauling her luggage out of the front seat.

"You must be Allegra's fiancé."

Mike set the suitcase down on the gravel. For a moment, he looked utterly blank, and Allegra wondered if her scheme was going to unravel before it even got off the ground, then he grinned and stepped forward to grip Tobias's hand. "Yep, that's me. Uh… Mike Callaghan's the name."

Tobias seemed ultra-relaxed. "The personal trainer. I saw you at the resort when I called in this afternoon."

A little shocked that Tobias knew Mike worked for her, when she was hoping that he would remain a mysterious figure, Allegra inserted herself into the conversation. "Mike doesn't work for the resort, he works for me. That's how we met."

She wound her arm through Mike's, and did her best to look as if she was happily relaxed and content to snuggle into her new fiancé's side. The situation was made all the more difficult by the fact that she was Mike's employer and, while he had agreed to act as her fiancé for money, the last thing she wanted to do was cross a line when it came to physical contact.

Tobias directed his next question at Mike. "How long have you worked at the spa?"

Mike froze like a deer in the headlights, and Allegra's stomach sank. She had briefed him extensively; she had just not thought he would need an actual script.

She smiled brightly. "He's been with the spa for a few weeks, isn't that right, Mike?"

"Uh—yeah. A few weeks."

Allegra kept the smile on her face. "It was a whirlwind…relationship." She could not quite say *engagement*.

Tobias crossed his arms over his chest. "Must have been." His gaze seemed to pin her in place. "I guess congratulations are in order. So, when is the happy day?"

Allegra glanced at her watch, in an effort to convey that she really did not have time for this chitchat. "We haven't gotten around to thinking about that just yet."

"Just like you haven't gotten around to getting a ring?"

Six

Allegra stiffened. Tobias's voice was neutral, but she knew him well enough to know that, when he was quiet, he was at his most dangerous. He had used that same kind of flat tone when he had ditched her. She had also heard it when he had queried Esmae's medical bill, which had sprouted one more zero than it should have had.

She had hoped to slide by without the necessity of a ring. Firstly, she could not really afford to buy one. After she paid Mike, her discretionary spending was gone for the next two months. Secondly, for Allegra, an engagement ring had always signified the promise of true love. It was bad enough that the engagement was a facade, she did not want to deepen the dishonesty of what she was doing by wearing a ring.

As loath as she was to give Tobias any information at all, she was left with no choice. She had planned for Mike to meet her in town tomorrow so she could pay him the first installment of his fee. She had also planned to get a ring. With any luck, she would be able to source a ring from the keepsakes Esmae had left her. Failing that, she could always use some of her own collection of fake and real diamonds, and have a ring made, but that would probably be almost as expensive as buying something new.

"As a matter of fact," she said smoothly, "we're planning on getting a ring tomorrow."

Feeling more cheerful, she released Mike's arm and tried not to look as relieved as she felt. "If you don't mind, we need to get on with moving my things into the house. I'm guessing I can use my old room?"

"Marta's already gotten it ready for you."

For the first time in days, a warm wave of pleasure washed through Allegra. Obviously, Tobias had kept on Marta Gomez, who had been Esmae's housekeeper and cook for a good thirty years, and her husband, Jose, who had looked after the grounds.

A burst of rap music made her start. Mike extracted his phone from his back pocket, and turned away to take the call. Long seconds passed as he strolled a few paces, then leaned against his truck, evidently in deep conversation.

Working to keep her expression smooth and unruffled, as if it didn't matter that her "fiancé" was now completely ignoring her, Allegra bent down into the car and dragged out the smaller of her two cases, which was wedged behind the seats. As she set it on the gravel and closed the car door, Tobias picked up the heavier case, which Mike had abandoned.

"Looks like your boyfriend's busy for a while. I'll show you to your room."

Following in Tobias's wake, Allegra walked into the familiar cool interior of the Spanish mansion, which his grandfather had built for Esmae. Classic blue-and-white mosaic tiles flowed into vaulting rooms. The dark, ornate furniture that Allegra remembered from her teen years was long gone, and in its place were rustic dressers and coffee tables, low couches upholstered in neutral linen, gorgeous chandeliers that looked as if they were made of translucent shells and thick comfortable floor rugs in neutrals and deep blues.

She followed Tobias up the long, sweeping staircase, with its soft white walls lined with Hunt family portraits. When she realized that he probably wouldn't deposit the bag at the door of her room, but would carry it in, a sudden tension gripped her.

Maybe she was being too sensitive now, but during the next month, her bedroom would be the only part of the house that was off-limits to Tobias. It would be her sanctuary. The last thing she needed was for him to invade her very private haven, so that every time she was in the room she had to fight off memories of his presence there.

She sped up, but he reached the doorway before her.

"Thanks very much for the help," she said briskly, "but you can leave my case in the hall—"

"While you wait for lover boy to carry it in?"

Ignoring her completely, Tobias strolled into the room and placed her suitcase at the foot of her bed.

To compound matters, as Allegra set the case she was carrying down, he walked over to a set of French doors, opened them and stepped out onto the balcony, which overlooked the drive. Jaw taut, she followed him, intending to order him out of her room.

Her stomach sank when she saw Mike below, still leaning on his truck and talking on his phone, a relaxed grin on his face, as if he had totally forgotten he was supposed to be helping her move in. As if he was enjoying talking to whomever was on the other end of the phone more than he enjoyed being with her.

Tobias lifted a brow. "Looks like Callaghan's still busy."

Probably with his real girlfriend.

That was a little detail Allegra had not yet had time to address. The first opportunity she got, she would make sure Mike understood that while he was employed as her fiancé, he could not have a girlfriend on the side.

Tobias's gaze shifted to her. "That's just as well, since I would prefer it if he didn't come upstairs into your bedroom."

"*You're* in my room."

"I'm not your lover."

And, suddenly, the air was alive with tension. Allegra was burningly aware that, if she'd thought Tobias had forgotten the night they had spent together, she was wrong.

He closed the gap between them, until he was close enough that she could feel the warmth of his body, smell the fresh scent of some expensive cologne. His gaze locked with hers. "Damn, I wasn't going to do this. Not yet, anyway."

She knew she should move. Alone with Tobias on the balcony, it was the perfect moment to take a stand and demonstrate that the old attraction that had held her in thrall for so long was now as dead as a doornail. The only problem was that, like the moments in the parking garage, knowing that Tobias still wanted her had done something crazy to her body. She felt frozen to the spot, yet burning and melting inside; she couldn't have moved if her life depended on it, because deep down, she realized that she didn't want to resist him. Just for once, she wanted to have what she wanted, and right now, that was Tobias.

She tilted her chin back and met his gaze boldly. "And what is it that you shouldn't do?"

"Kiss you," he ground out. "Not with him here."

Warm, calloused hands cupped her face, sending further fiery shivers of sensation through her. The calluses reminded her that Tobias was not just a high-powered executive running a multi-national empire. Apart from his time in the military, he had always spent a lot of time in and on the water. When she had vacationed with Esmae, she had used to watch him obsessively as he had sailed yachts in the bay.

Tobias's mouth closed over hers. White heat

burned through her, and she found herself going up on her toes, her arms automatically looping around his neck as she fitted herself against his body and melted into the kiss.

This shouldn't feel so familiar, she thought breathlessly.

And it shouldn't feel so good.

Tobias groaned, which sent another hot thrill through her, lifted his head, then settled back down for a second, deeper kiss and memories she had suppressed for two long years flooded back.

The brazen way she had thrown caution to the winds and virtually seduced Tobias.

She had found the spare key to Esmae's beach house, which was kept under a potted plant, and they had stumbled into the darkened hall. Switching one light on, and leaving the rest of the house in dimness, she had taken Tobias's hand and led him to the stairs. Several long, drugging kisses later, they had located a bedroom. As they undressed and fell together on a muslin-swathed four-poster bed, moonlight had flooded through the French doors, investing what they were doing with an otherworldly romanticism that had added to the sense that what was happening wasn't quite real.

But the sharp memory of what had happened just two days later put the lovemaking in context. It had been casual sex. Nothing more, nothing less, and that was exactly where this was heading.

Aware that they had been brazenly kissing on the balcony, in full view of Mike, she jerked free of Tobias's hold. Not that Mike had noticed. At that precise moment, he finally finished his call, looked around, then up, and grinned and waved.

If ever there was a moment that Allegra reflected on why she didn't feel the slightest attraction for Mike, that was it. If she had any dragons to slay, he just wouldn't be there. He would be phoning one of his girlfriends or talking to his agent, and she would have to take care of business herself.

Feeling suddenly annoyed beyond belief and *suspicious*, she met Tobias's gaze squarely. "Why did you kiss me?" She lowered her voice, just in case Mike could hear. "No, don't answer, because I *know* why. You wanted to see if I was here to seduce you into a marriage that neither of us in our most insane moments would ever want. I would just like to reiterate that, despite the kiss, which was totally inappropriate and dishonorable on your part because I am *engaged*, I do not want you."

Tobias folded his arms across his chest, his gaze oddly brooding. "I wasn't testing you."

"Then what were you doing?"

A knock on the door brought the conversation to an abrupt halt.

Marta poked her head around the door, her expression openly curious. "I'm just about to leave now, but I've left dinner for you. All you need to do is serve yourselves."

Half an hour later, after Mike had driven away, Tobias walked downstairs and out onto the drive to lock his truck. He was on his way back to the house when he saw a set of folded papers where Mike's truck had been parked. He picked them up. He wasn't interested in snooping, but in this case, he didn't need to be, because the sheets were folded in such a way that the words were on the outside, and clearly visible.

Dating Schedule.

Tobias gave up any idea of discretion and perused both printouts, which were produced in a spreadsheet format. There were a series of preplanned dates, instructions on where to meet, what to wear and, several times the bolded command that Mike was not to pick Allegra up in his rusted old truck, because she would be doing the driving.

Apparently, when it came to dating, Allegra liked to take the lead, and Mike didn't just need direction, he needed micromanaging, even down to instructions on what to wear for specific dates.

He ran his eye over the dating schedule, which was top heavy on activities that centered on the Ocean Beach Resort and seemed to have more to do with Callaghan cleaning out some shed filled with old gym equipment than with actual romantic interludes. Tobias was pretty sure that the other address that figured prominently was the site for Allegra's second proposed spa property. Those dates seemed to involve a tape measure and meetings with an engineer. There was no mention of the kind of romantic dates that would be paramount for an engaged couple except for one sketchy date that was simply labeled, *I get the ring. Lunch, Atraeus Mall, twelve sharp.*

He presumed that was about getting the engagement ring. Although, it sounded like Allegra was providing her own ring, and Callaghan was turning up, as ordered, for lunch. And nowhere was there any mention of meetings with either Allegra's or Callaghan's families.

While he knew that her family was based in New Orleans, he knew nothing about Callaghan except that he worked for Allegra. *Although that would soon change*, he thought grimly.

Refolding the schedule, he carried it with him into the house. When he reached the library, which housed his grandfather's collection of rare books, an enormous carved mahogany desk and a couple of leather chesterfield couches that looked like they'd come off of a period movie set, he slipped the papers into a drawer.

The portrait of his great-grandfather, Jebediah Hunt, with his granite features and straight black brows, seemed to stare down at him. Not for the first time, Tobias noted that he looked stern and unlikeable, not the kind of character he would want to meet in a darkened alley.

Allegra's words about Alexandra leaving Jebediah, because she had just not liked him, came back to haunt him. It was a fact that his great-grandfather had been a tough and difficult man.

Tobias had to wonder if Allegra saw *him* in the same light. His grandfather had used to tell him he was a chip off the old block, referring to Jebediah as the "old block." Now Tobias was beginning to think the words had been a criticism, not a compliment.

But, for all his faults, Jeb had not lacked character. When things had gone south with Alexandra and the ranch, he had walked off the land and started again, this time as a Pinkerton agent. A few years later, he had started his own detective agency, which had been the beginnings of Hunt Security.

Tobias walked to the French doors that opened onto a patio. The view of the Atlantic Ocean from the high point the mansion commanded was impressive, although it barely impinged on his thoughts.

Ever since this morning, when Allegra had told him she was engaged, he had been tense and on edge, but now he was almost certain her engagement was fake. Especially since the fiancé she had produced out of the blue was an employee. But he was also aware that he couldn't risk making that assumption.

He slid his phone out of his pocket and made a call to the head of the Miami branch of Hunt Private Investigations. Tulley picked up almost immediately. Minutes later, Tobias terminated the call.

If Allegra had hired Mike to play her fiancé, Tobias had to assume she had done so to either make it look as if she hadn't influenced the will and was an innocent party in Esmae's machinations, or she was trying to protect herself from him.

Given that Allegra had no compunction about putting him in his place, he did not think the second reason applied.

Of course, he couldn't rule out the possibility that he had gotten the situation completely wrong, and the engagement was real.

Although, he didn't think so.

Just the thought of Allegra with Callaghan made his jaw tighten. Every instinct told him that, despite the engagement, they weren't lovers, yet.

The dynamic did seem more employer-and-employee than lovers, but he couldn't take the risk.

He had given Tulley twenty-four hours to investigate Callaghan, but whatever the PI uncovered, Tobias was already decided.

Callaghan had to go.

Seven

Allegra closed the door of her bedroom behind her and leaned on it, her heart racing.

She touched her mouth, which was still faintly swollen and tingling. She couldn't believe she had let Tobias kiss her, *in full view of Mike, while he had been taking a call down on the drive.*

If Mike had turned his head by just an inch or two and looked up, he would have seen them, then the whole engagement scenario would have become… complicated.

A flashback to the moment Tobias's mouth had come down on hers made her tense. Suddenly, it seemed unbearably hot, the air humid and close. Pushing away from the door, she walked through to her en suite bathroom and splashed cold water on her face. After blotting her face dry, she hung up the thick, luxurious hand towel and checked her appearance in case she had smudged her mascara, which she had.

Using one of the cleansing pads Marta always kept the bathrooms supplied with, she cleaned away the dark smudges and took stock. Unfortunately, her mouth still looked faintly swollen, and there was a small red mark on her jaw, as if Tobias's five-o'clock shadow had grazed her skin.

Awareness tightened her stomach as she remembered the shiver of pleasure that had gone through her when he had done just that. To add to the picture of wanton abandonment, her neatly coiled hair had come loose to the point of collapse, and tendrils were wisping around her chin and clinging to her neck.

Dimly, she noted that was probably because Tobias's fingers had slid through her hair as he had cupped the back of her head while he had kissed her.

While *they* had kissed, she corrected bleakly. Tobias had moved in on her, but she couldn't forget that she had kissed him back with enthusiasm.

As if she couldn't get enough of him.

Forcibly tamping down her thoughts about Tobias, she returned to the bedroom, unzipped her case, and found her makeup case and the waterproof bag that contained her hair and skincare products.

Setting the cosmetic bags down on the beautiful oyster marble bathroom counter, she systematically unpacked, taking a simple pleasure in stocking the bathroom with all of the signature products of Madison Spas. Storing the empty cases in the vanity cabinet, she dragged the pins from her hair, brushed it out until it was smooth, then redid the smooth coil at her nape.

After dabbing concealer over the red mark, she smoothed on a tinted moisturizer, then touched up with a hint of blusher. A coat of mascara on her lashes and a quick colorless gloss on her lips finished off the transformation.

Walking back out to the bedroom, she unpacked her clothes, a process she hoped would normalize being in the same house as Tobias.

Unfortunately, feeling normal, when she had kissed him, not once, but *twice* in one day, was proving difficult.

The dire warnings one of her counselors had given her about the dangerous flaws inherent in burying what had happened between her and Tobias with an organized list of therapies, as if, cumulatively, they guaranteed a cure, came back to haunt her.

In a moment of clarity, she realized that the problem was that, underneath it all, she *liked* the challenge Tobias posed. He was exactly the kind of tall, muscular, brooding alpha guy she naturally gravitated toward. The second she stepped into the same room as Tobias, her heart sped up and adrenaline pumped.

The plain fact was, she had been brought up with wolves, and she had gotten used to running with them. If she had been able to wind Tobias around her little finger, she would have lost interest in him, the way she had with other men.

She took a deep breath and let it out slowly.

The thought that she might weaken and give in to the attraction that still drew her to Tobias, and which seemed just as powerfully at work in him, briefly transfixed her.

It wouldn't happen, she reassured herself. That was precisely why she had a fake fiancé.

Allegra grabbed a fragile, filmy dress in a vibrant jungle print with a plunging neckline—another extremely expensive Messena original—and shoved it on a hanger.

All she had to do was manage her time so that she did not spend it with Tobias, and stick to the engagement program.

A great way to stay away from him tonight would be to look for the keepsakes Esmae had left her, and see if there was anything that remotely resembled an engagement ring. According to Marta, the antique trinket box her great-aunt had reserved for her was labeled with her name and stored somewhere in the attic of the beach house.

Returning to the bedroom, she transferred the remaining clothing into drawers and the gorgeous walk-in closet. The final item was her jewelry case. However, as she lifted it out of the suitcase, she realized that the steel catch had gotten caught in the stretchy webbing, which had secured her suits. The net result was that the box, which was *heavy*, slipped from her fingers and hit the floor. The lid sprung open and diamonds and pageant bling for Africa spilled across the floor.

Muttering beneath her breath, she returned all of the items to the box, taking care to store the genuine diamonds in their own special compartment. However, when she tried to close it, the lid wouldn't fasten properly, because the catch was now broken. She would either have to buy a new box, or get this one repaired.

She placed the jewelry case on a shelf in the closet, then neatly stored her cases away in there, as well. Her few dresses and outfits looked sparse and insignificant on their hangers, but that was a welcome reminder that her stay here would be short.

All she had to do was sleep in the beautiful king-size bed, eat the delicious meals that Marta left and locate the personal belongings that Esmae had stored in the beach house.

As heart-wrenching as it would feel to go through her aunt's personal things, she could not contain a certain buzz of excitement. The mysterious "keepsakes" aside, there was a painting of Alexandra Mallory, the interesting and mysterious ancestor Allegra had only ever heard about, but never seen.

Dinner was brief, and oddly anticlimactic. Allegra had expected that Tobias might try to engage her in conversation, so she had pointedly been busy on her phone. However, aside from an initial greeting, Tobias had practically ignored her, eating the fresh crab appetizer followed by one of Marta's spicy steak salads in between calls. Allegra had just found the cold dessert Marta had left in the fridge when Tobias had taken yet another call.

As he got up from the table, Allegra heard the name, Francesca, and froze.

Closing the fridge door, she walked out to the gorgeous dining room, which opened onto a terrace. She slapped the chilled bowl of dessert down on the solid oak server that ran along one wall as Tobias walked out onto the sun-washed terrace to take the call, in private.

Allegra spooned a small amount of the fresh fruit salad into a glass bowl, all while trying to convince herself that he couldn't possibly be talking to Francesca Messena.

Correction, Francesca Atraeus, because she was now married. But when she moved closer to the terrace, ostensibly to look at the view, she heard Tobias mention the name John, Francesca's tycoon husband, and all doubt evaporated.

An odd pastiche of emotions gripped her. Shock, and a sinking feeling that Francesca was *still* in contact with Tobias despite choosing and marrying someone else, followed by burning outrage.

How could Tobias kiss her *twice*—and both times it had been a whole lot more than a kiss—then have a private, intimate chat with his ex-lover?

And what did Francesca Atraeus think she was doing? Wasn't one man enough for her?

The burst of anger gave way to a hollow feeling in the pit of her stomach that she recognized all too well, because she had felt the same empty feeling when she had found out that Tobias had gone straight from her bed to Francesca's.

She stared at her dessert. As tempting as the jewel-bright fruits looked, she was no longer hungry. Walking back to the table, she set the bowl, and her dessert fork, down. A sip of water relieved some of the tension in her throat but didn't shift the churning sensation in her stomach.

Two years ago, when she had learned that Tobias had gone back to Francesca, she had done some research and discovered an interesting fact, courtesy of his lover's social media pages. Francesca liked men, plural, and had gone through boyfriends like a hot knife through butter. But most of her exes were still in contact with her.

Either Francesca was the nicest person alive, or she enjoyed the power of keeping men on a string.

The low, clipped timbre of Tobias's voice grew louder, signaling that he was strolling back in the direction of the dining room. If she didn't know better, she would think it was a business conversation, but, as far as she knew, Tobias didn't have any business connections with Francesca, who was a fashion designer. That pointed to a possibility that made her jaw tighten: that Francesca, despite her marriage, still wanted Tobias.

When Tobias came back to the table, Allegra picked up her fork and tried to look interested in the fruit salad. "Business call?"

His expression was remote as he took his seat directly opposite her. "I thought you didn't want to talk."

She knew she should leave it, but somehow the fact that Tobias was talking to the woman he had dated before and after he had slept with her, *less than an hour after he had kissed her on the balcony*, was infuriating. It underlined the fact that, when it came to Tobias, she had always been in the shadow of another woman.

Picking up the dessert fork, she stabbed a piece of melon and attempted the smooth, professional smile she usually reserved for difficult clients. "I thought I heard the name Francesca."

"Francesca Atraeus. That's right. She's arriving on a flight tomorrow."

Allegra froze "She's coming *here*?"

"Is that a problem?"

Allegra abandoned the fork with its mangled piece of melon. "It is if she's coming to stay at this house, since I wasn't allowed to have Mike stay."

Tobias frowned. "Francesca's not staying here. Why would she, when she can stay at her husband's hotel?"

Allegra blinked. In the heat of the moment, she had forgotten that John Atraeus owned one of the swankiest hotels in town, so Francesca could stay there any time she liked. Not to mention the fact that she also had family in town.

The problem was, the instant Tobias had mentioned Francesca's name she had felt a weird sense of déjà vu. She had kissed Tobias, twice. That morning they had come crazily close to making love, *so of course Tobias was going to sleep with Francesca again.*

She took a deep breath and tried to think, although thinking was difficult when all she wanted to do was reach across the table, snatch up Tobias's phone, fling it over the terrace and watch it break into pieces.

With an effort of will, she dialed back on an anger that, after two years of counseling and calming therapies, should not exist. The kind of explosive anger she recognized all too well because she had felt it once before, when Tobias had left her bed and gone back to Francesca's.

She was jealous. Burningly, crazily jealous.

Allegra stared at the tough line of Tobias's jaw. She needed to go somewhere quiet and bang her head against something hard, something that would hurt. Somehow, she had once more allowed herself to become entangled in the old fatal attraction: she was back to wanting Tobias, again.

"So, why, exactly, is *she*—" she couldn't bring herself to say Francesca's name "—coming to Miami?"

Tobias, who had resumed eating his beef salad, as if nothing momentous had happened, paused. "Does it matter?"

Allegra kept her expression smooth and neutral with difficulty. "I wouldn't have asked if it didn't matter."

He set his fork down. "Her twin was interested in installing one of their boutiques at the Ocean Beach

Resort. Since Sophie now has to be out of town for a couple of weeks, Francesca agreed to come and check the resort out."

Allegra took a sip of water while she tried to come to terms with the fact that Francesca could be a regular visitor at Ocean Beach. A regular part of Tobias's life, even though she was married. "The resort doesn't have space for another clothing boutique."

Then a horrifying thought occurred.

She pinned him with a fiery glance. "Unless you're planning on not renewing my lease when it expires in two month's time."

And of course, she suddenly knew that was *exactly* what he was planning. She had been so absorbed with navigating the terms of the will, and getting through this month with Tobias, that she'd sidelined the issue of the lease. But, if he wanted to get rid of her completely, she couldn't think of a more perfect way.

"The reason the Messena twins are looking at the Ocean Beach Resort is that they know we're looking at expanding."

Allegra frowned, aware that Tobias had failed to answer her question about the lease, but she was now sidetracked by this new issue. "That's the first I've heard of it."

"That's because nothing's decided yet. At the moment, expanding the resort is at the planning stage."

Even though she knew she was overreacting, she couldn't seem to stop herself. "But you had time to tell Francesca."

Tobias's cool glance seemed to laser through her. The intensity of it made her suddenly aware that she had been just a little too transparent about the other woman; that she could even have made the mistake of letting him know she was jealous.

Just as quickly, she dismissed the notion. They were talking about the resort; she was worried about the future of her business. There was no way Tobias could know that she was becoming more and more annoyed about his relationship with Francesca.

"As a matter of fact," he said quietly. "Esmae had had tentative plans to expand, which she'd put on hold when she got unwell. Her banker, Gabriel Messena, brought up the project at the funeral. I gave him permission to mention that there could be retail premises becoming available in the next year to his sisters. Is that a problem?"

Allegra plastered a smooth, professional smile on her face. "Why would it be a problem?"

Briskly, she pushed to her feet. Picking up her dessert dish, she aimed a neutral look in Tobias's general direction, as if everything was perfectly fine. "If you'll excuse me, I'm going to have a look in the beach house attic while it's still light out. According to Marta, that's where Esmae stored the items she wanted me to have."

As Allegra walked up the stairs to her bedroom, she acknowledged that the fact that Francesca Messena was still in Tobias's life, and still wanted him, shouldn't be a problem.

But, now that she had acknowledged that she wanted Tobias, it was a *big* problem.

Until Allegra received evidence to the contrary, she had to assume that Francesca, despite her marriage to John Atraeus, had once again set her sights on Tobias.

Two years ago, Francesca had gotten Tobias, and Allegra had let him go. But that would be happening again over her dead body.

It occurred to her that she could not go after Tobias and keep her fake engagement to Mike.

She would have to choose.

A fake fiancé who was extremely expensive and who had to be cued at every turn? Or a frustrating, elusive, battle-scarred tycoon who was making no bones about the fact that he wanted her in his bed, at least for now?

And she would have to make her choice before Francesca landed in Miami.

Eight

Allegra took the path down the hill to the beach house as the sun finally set and the long, extended twilight settled in. Flicking on her phone light, she negotiated the final set of steps and climbed onto the deck of the beach house, which was located on a steep bank that overlooked the beach. She found the key to the back door, which was concealed beneath a potted plant, and paused for a moment, because it had been so long since she had ventured anywhere near the beach house. Unlocking the door, she stepped into the small hall.

Wrinkling her nose at the stuffy heat, she flicked on a light to relieve the gloom, and left the door open to let fresh air circulate through the house. Sliding her phone into a handy pocket in her dress, she did a quick walk through an equally hot-and-stuffy kitchen, dining and sitting room area, and decided to open a set of French doors to allow the sea breeze to flow through.

For once, she was unable to appreciate the breath-taking view of the ocean stretching to a hazy horizon and, off to the right, the pier, with its dinghy floating off a rope at the end. If it was this stifling downstairs, the attic would be like an oven. Taking a last deep breath of fresh air, she headed upstairs, flicking lights on as she went.

Despite her every effort, her heart sped up as she walked past the master bedroom, with its wrought iron four-poster bed—draped in filmy mosquito netting—dark floorboards and bleached woven rugs. Two years had passed since she'd spent the night with Tobias here. She had expected it to look different but, disorientingly, it all looked exactly the same.

Dragging her gaze from the bed, she flicked on a hall light, dispelling the sense of being caught in the past, and entangled in memories that were still too vivid. However, as she started up the narrow flight of stairs that led up to the attic, the wall sconce made a suspicious buzzing sound, flickered, then died.

She muttered beneath her breath because, when she had switched on that last light, it must have been too much for the antiquated system, and now she had blown a fuse, plunging the entire upstairs into darkness. Reaching into her pocket, she found her phone. Moments later, she activated the flashlight app again and a reassuring beam of white light illuminated the door to the attic.

She had only ever been up here once before, when Esmae had asked her to bring down a box of clothing she had wanted to donate to charity. As she stepped into the dusty, vaulted room, striped with shadows, courtesy of the window shutters, a curious sense of expectation assailed her. Even though she was a Mallory, and knew the basic story of what had gone wrong between Alexandra and Jebediah, actual facts were sketchy. And, while she had seen sepia photos of her grandparents, she had never glimpsed a picture of Alexandra or her husband, James Walter Mallory, who had died before Alexandra had left England.

She flicked a light switch. Of course, nothing happened.

She beamed the light from her phone around the room as she picked her way through old tea chests and broken furniture. Dust made her cough as she brushed past furniture that had probably not been touched for decades. She found the catches of the shutters and, systematically, opened them to allow the last natural light of the day to lighten the gloom, and took stock.

Apparently, Esmae's personal family items, for convenience, were situated close to the door. Almost instantly, Allegra spotted an old dresser shoved up against the wall. A small wooden box sat on top of it.

In order to reach the dresser, she had to skirt a broken armchair and clamber across what looked like an ancient travelling trunk. The second she touched the box, which had a small white label on it bearing her name, a small pulse of excitement went through her.

She brushed her palm over the smooth surface of the lid. As she cleaned the dust off, the nascent gleam of the letter *A* inset in mother-of-pearl in the fine, dark wood, sent another small thrill through her. This must have been Alexandra's personal jewelry box.

Out of nowhere, emotion washed through her, strong enough that she even felt faintly teary, which was unusual since she hadn't expected to feel much of a connection. After all, she had never met Alexandra Mallory, and most of what she'd learned had left a conflicting impression.

She hefted the box, which was surprisingly heavy, and decided to carry it downstairs where she could clean it up, wash her hands, then examine the contents in the light.

Several minutes later, she set the box down on the kitchen counter. After washing the dust from her hands, she checked out the kitchen cupboards. Esmae had always kept the kitchen fully stocked with cleaning products and basic items, just in case someone came to stay, so there was no problem finding paper towels and hand wash.

As she wiped away the remaining dust that coated the box, the quality of it became clear. Allegra couldn't be sure, but the dark, swirling wood looked like rosewood, and the mother-of-pearl inlay wasn't just confined to the letter *A*, but was used as a decorative edging and for a delicate filigree of flowers that encircled the *A* and flowed around the box.

Throwing the soiled paper towels in the trash, she unlatched the silver catch and opened the lid. She didn't know what she expected to find, but the faded diary sitting on top wasn't it.

She removed the diary and found a series of worn black velvet bags. She opened the first one and a fiery necklace flowed into her palm. She was no expert, but from the color shooting off the clear crystals, she was pretty sure they were diamonds. Although, she couldn't really tell in this light. She would have to examine them in the morning, and get them properly assessed by a jeweler.

If they were diamonds, that just didn't make sense. She knew how the story went. Alexandra and Esmae were both supposed to have been broke.

Who lost everything but held onto the family jewels?

The remaining bags contained matching earrings, a brooch, a bracelet and a stunning ring. There were also simpler, prettier pieces, comprised of pearls and garnets, that looked like they belonged to an older time, the gold heavy and gleaming, the settings blurred.

Feeling more than a little confused, because she hadn't known that this jewelry even existed, and Esmae had never breathed a word, Allegra carefully replaced all of the items. She could only assume that her aunt had inherited the jewelry at some point but, because she had married an incredibly wealthy Hunt, she had stowed it away rather than wear something that might be contentious.

But that still didn't explain why Esmae had never spoken about it, or why it had all been left up here, to molder in a dusty attic.

Leaving the box on the counter, she made her way through the dim house and climbed back up to the attic to see if she could locate the painting of Alexandra. She was in the middle of clambering across an old sofa when a scraping sound made her freeze. Her first thought was that she had disturbed rats, in which case she was leaving *now*; then the low, gravelly timbre of Tobias's voice registered.

"Damn, what's happened to the lights?"

Allegra stepped on something that shifted under her foot, a moldering pile of magazines. Luckily, she was still holding onto the back of the sofa, so she kept her balance. "I think I blew a fuse when I switched on the hall light."

A beam of light briefly pinned her. "When you didn't return to the house, I thought something must have happened. I'll check out the fuse box in the morning. If it's still the old, antiquated system my grandfather had put in, the whole thing probably needs replacing." He swept his phone light around the room. "Damn, didn't Esmae throw anything away?"

"Apparently not. And neither did anyone else." She held up what looked like an ancient cattle whip. "I'm thinking this didn't belong to Esmae."

"Let's hope not."

She caught the gleam of a wicked grin, quickly gone, and for a moment, her heart stopped in her chest. She had seen Tobias laugh and smile before, but it had always been for others, never for her.

Tobias dragged the huge old horsehair sofa she had just scaled aside. The next obstacle was a large and hideous armchair that was leaking stuffing.

He hefted the chair as if it weighed nothing, propping it on top of an old mattress. "About time most of this stuff went in a dumpster."

Dust swirled in the air, making her sneeze, but at least he had cleared a path. "Thanks, I think." She found herself smiling in Tobias's direction, which was faintly shocking, because in all the years she had known him, she didn't think they had ever shared this kind of light banter.

"No problem. Looks like Esmae stored a good three generations of junk up here. It's going to take weeks to clear it all out."

Tobias beamed his phone light into the corner. "Is that what you're looking for?"

Allegra glimpsed the outline of a painting, covered by a sheet and propped against the wall. Her heart sped up. If she didn't miss her guess, that was Alexandra's portrait.

"That would be four generations of junk," she said softly.

Dragging the dustcover aside, she shone her light on the painting and caught her breath. Apart from the fact that Alexandra's skin was pale and her hair was darker than Allegra's—and the time period was Victorian—it was eerily like looking into a mirror.

Her great-grandmother had clearly been painted when she was young, possibly before she had married. Her smile was warm and faintly mischievous, as if she was on the edge of dissolving into laughter, and there was a sparkle in her very direct gaze. Allegra hadn't expected to feel any kind of a connection with her ancestor, but the painting was so lifelike and vivid that it seemed to bridge the gap of years.

Allegra checked out Alexandra's hands in the painting. There was no ring, so she was definitely painted before she had married. She also noted that while Alexandra was wearing some of the older, more ornate garnet-and-pearl jewelry from the box, there wasn't a diamond in sight.

Tobias's phone light joined with hers, bringing out the Titian glow of Alexandra's hair, the gleam of her eyes and the exotic cut to her cheekbones, as if somewhere along the line she had Italian blood flowing through her veins. "She's beautiful."

An unexpected glow of happiness flooded her as Allegra attempted to lift the painting up, in order to move it closer to the attic door. If Tobias thought Alexandra—who looked remarkably like herself—was beautiful, then, by definition, he must also think that she was beautiful.

"I'll get that." Tobias lifted the heavy painting from her hands as if it weighed almost nothing and propped it by the attic door. "No wonder Jebediah wanted to marry her."

Allegra frowned. "That's the first I've heard of that."

Tobias made his way across the attic to the nearest window. He yanked at a catch that had stuck, and eventually got the window open. A cooling breeze relieved the heat. "They were sleeping together, and he had plans to marry her. That was the reason he went into business with her."

Indignation rose in Allegra. "Last I heard, sleeping with a man isn't part of a business contract, unless—"

"She agreed to the marriage," Tobias said bleakly. "Then, practically the next day a city lawyer turned up and Alexandra and her two children disappeared. No explanations, no goodbyes. The lawyer wrote from New York to terminate the business relationship and the rest is history."

Suddenly, the animosity between the Hunts and the Mallorys was beginning to make more sense. It hadn't all been about the oil well; it had been *personal*.

Allegra stared at the fresh-faced portrait of a young lady with a firm chin and a remarkably steady gaze. Allegra hadn't dwelled overmuch on the conflicted history of the Hunts and the Mallorys, but in her opinion, Alexandra didn't look anything like a gold-digger. "It sounds like we have two different stories. Mine says that my great-grandmother who was left on her own after her husband died, brought up two children who turned out to be successful, functional human beings. When the money ran out, she died poor and still alone. I don't know what happened between them, but Jebediah must have gotten it wrong." But, even as she said the words, she couldn't forget the cache of diamonds in the jewelry box downstairs.

"Whether he got it wrong or not," Tobias said on a flat, hard note, "it was Jebediah who got hurt."

Her gaze clashed with his. "But he clearly recovered and married, while Alexandra never did. Explain that. And, if she was so beautiful and so focused on the bottom line, why go to bed with a ranch hand? For that matter, why go into business with him? It doesn't make sense. The obvious solution for a woman who wanted riches was to marry someone with a fortune."

"Is that what you would do?"

The words seemed to drop into the well of the night, and suddenly the conversation was deeply, unbearably personal. Years of hurt coalesced into a hard bands across her chest. She had lost count of the times men, in general, had seen her as on the hunt for a rich husband, or trivialized her because she was a woman and attractive. For Tobias to do it was the last straw.

"That would be no and no." Dragging in a deep breath, she tried to dial down the tension that was humming through her. It registered that half the problem was that it was so hot and humid and dusty in the attic that it was hard to breathe. Deciding to leave the painting where it was and get it another day, she stepped through the door and started down the pitch-black stairs, her trusty phone with its light beaming ahead of her.

She was aware of the click of the attic door closing, Tobias's tread on the stairs behind her, and suddenly she was sick and tired of being treated like a cheap opportunist, and spoiling for a fight. When she reached the hall landing, she spun and jabbed a finger at his chest. "I don't know how you can make a comment like that. You don't know the first thing about me. I didn't get a business degree because I wanted to sit at home doing my nails while some man goes out and provides for me. I prefer to create my own business opportunities and make my own money."

Something flashed in Tobias's gaze. "And keep your men controllable. Like Mike."

Her brows drew together. There was something fundamentally wrong with the conversation. First she was some kind of cliché gold-digger looking for a man to take care of her. Now, apparently, she was domineering. "What makes you think Mike's controllable?"

"He is your employee."

"And you think I'd hold that over his head?"

"It's not the kind of relationship I'd be aiming for."

"Now I'm interested," she shot back. "Tell me what the perfect relationship looks like, since, clearly I haven't stumbled across it yet."

Tobias's hand landed on the wall beside her head. Suddenly, he was close enough that she could smell the clean scent of his skin and the subtle hint of an expensive aftershave. "You need someone who won't take orders."

"Last I heard you're not even close to a love doctor." She drew a lungful of air and lifted her chin, but that was a mistake, because it brought her mouth closer to his. "Got someone in mind?"

Something heated and unbearably familiar flashed in his gaze. Wrong question. She had practically issued an invitation.

"Now that you mention it," he said flatly, "that would be me."

Nine

Heat flooded Allegra, almost welding her to the spot. She met Tobias's gaze boldly. "I thought you didn't want a relationship."

"It's more that I don't want to want one," he ground out.

"That makes it worse!"

His head dipped, and she felt the edge of his teeth on one lobe. Sensation arced through her. The passionate moments on her bedroom balcony replayed through her mind. She needed to move, *now*. The conversation had gotten too personal and, when it came to Tobias, her willpower wasn't good. This close, she was reminded of the night they'd spent together, of how good it had felt before everything had gone so horribly wrong.

She drew back. "What makes you think I still want you?"

"This." He brushed his mouth across hers.

She drew an impeded breath. "That's not fair."

Tobias picked up a strand of hair and wound it around his finger, tugging lightly. "Believe me, if I could control whatever it is that happens to me when you're around, I would."

That wasn't what she wanted to hear, that she was someone he was unwillingly attracted to, rather than someone he could have a genuine relationship with. But, along with the hurt, there was a glimmer of light at the end of a long, dark corridor. "But you do want me."

And, ever since they'd first slept together, he hadn't been able to stop wanting her. It wasn't much, it wasn't enough, but it was *something*.

"Six years now, and counting."

Her breath came in. She had expected him to say two years, not six.

Six years ago, she'd had her first holiday in Miami. It had been a gift from Esmae to celebrate the successful completion of her first year at Stanford. It had also been the start of her crush on Tobias, who, at that point, had used to keep his yacht moored off the end of Esmae's pier. Allegra had used to sit on the beach with her sunglasses and a magazine and try to pretend that she wasn't fascinated and a little heartsick that Tobias always had his beautiful blond girlfriend in tow.

Her aunt had been kind enough to invite her back

during subsequent summer breaks. In all of that time, Tobias, who had always been cool and distant, had barely seemed to notice her. Until they had ended up sitting on the same log at a beach party that had followed the more formal birthday party Esmae had thrown.

She planted her palms on the warm, hard muscle of his chest. "Then why did you walk away after our night together? Don't tell me it was because of the Jebediah and Alexandra thing."

"To be honest, that never entered my mind—"

"Because it doesn't apply to us," she said fiercely "It never has."

He pulled her close, and she let him, suddenly needing to feel that the wanting was real.

"I'd broken up with Lindsay a couple of weeks earlier—"

"The tall, blond girl you were engaged to?"

And, suddenly, she got it. He had said six years, which meant he had wanted her *while* he had been in a relationship with Lindsay. She frowned, because that meant she had been the "other woman" for Lindsay, which wasn't cool. Not that she had known it! "And you felt guilty because you wanted me."

"Something like that."

She registered that there was more that he wasn't telling her, but it was hard to concentrate on what that could be when she was so thrilled that he had genuinely wanted her for *six* years. She was on the verge of probing into what, exactly, that *more* could be, when he leaned down and kissed her and the question dissolved.

Lifting up on her toes, she angled her jaw to deepen the kiss, looped her arms around his neck and fitted herself more closely against him. His instant response sent a wave of heat through her.

She registered his hands on her waist, then they were moving, one step backward, through a doorway. Even though it was dark, and the phone lights were not much help, if she didn't miss her guess, this was the bedroom they had made love in last time. Two more steps, and she felt the soft but firm outline of a bed at the back of her knees.

Tobias lifted his head, but she pulled his mouth back to hers and kissed him again, long enough that she felt she was drowning in sensation. His hands settled at her waist, then glided up her back. She felt her dress slacken as her zipper glided down. Flimsy cotton puddled around her feet on the floor. By the time she had stepped out of it, Tobias had dispensed with her bra.

She dragged at the buttons of his shirt and found naked skin, and the intriguing roughness of the hair sprinkled across his chest. With an impatient movement, he finished the job, shrugged out of the garment and let it fall to the floor. His hands closed around her breasts, sending heated sensation zinging through her. He dipped his head and took one nipple into his mouth, and time seemed to slow, then stop, as heat gathered and coiled tight.

"Oh, no you don't," he said huskily.

A split second later, the room went sideways as he swung her up into his arms. Dimly, she registered that one of her sneakers had slipped off her foot, while the other was still on, then the coolness of the linen coverlet sent a faint shiver through her as he set her down on the soft expanse of the daybed.

Outside, the wind, which had picked up, sent rain scattering against the windows. But in the darkened room, illuminated only by their phone lights, it still felt close and overly warm.

Feeling suddenly vulnerable and exposed, despite not quite being naked, she toed off her remaining sneaker and watched as Tobias peeled out of his pants. Light and shadow flowed over his broad shoulders, tiger-striping his muscled torso and narrow hips, and her breath came in at his raw, masculine beauty. Dimly, she registered that Tobias had just sheathed himself with a condom. The fact that he carried condoms on him made her go still inside. Maybe he was just careful, and they were not for anyone specific. But the fact that he had them on hand pointed out the obvious, that Tobias was a sexually active male.

The thought that the condoms could be for Francesca Messena made her stiffen. If she'd had any doubts about making love with Tobias, they were gone in that moment. Francesca might have plans for Tobias, but right now, he was *hers*.

Six years ago, Allegra had taken one look at Tobias, her mind had gone blank and her body had reacted. It had been chemistry, pure and simple, and the plain fact was she had never fully recovered from it.

Somehow, despite all of the work she had done to move on, the attraction had lingered and she had become ensnared by it again.

But then, so had Tobias.

The bed dipped as Tobias came down beside her. She wound her arms around his neck and snuggled close, her breath coming in at the intimate heat of skin on skin.

A long drugging kiss later, and she lifted her hips so he could strip her panties down her legs, then there was no time to think. She grasped his shoulders as he slowly entered her. Then, she shifted a little, trying to ease the pressure, because it had been two years since they had made love. Two years, during which she hadn't wanted to be intimate with anyone.

And before that? Well, she just hadn't been intimate with anyone. She had been too driven, too busy and too annoyed with the expectation that she should have sex with a guy just because *they* wanted it. Consequently, the experience was still weirdly new.

His gaze locked with hers as he seated himself fully inside her. "Are you okay?"

She grasped his shoulders and braced herself, every cell taut and tingling as he began to move. "I'm fine." She drew an impeded breath. "You're wearing a condom, which is good, because I do not want to be an unwed mother. Just…don't stop."

And, right there, he stopped.

She caught the gleam of a wry smile. "Do you always like to be in charge?"

"Of course, I like to be in charge," she muttered. "I'm from Louisiana."

This time he definitely grinned, as if it was cute that she was from Louisiana. He should meet her mother. She frowned when he still didn't move. She wriggled a bit closer. What *was* the holdup?

Inspiration struck. She had read *a lot* about nipples. Apparently, you could control men when you touched them. So, she touched them.

He made a sound somewhere between a strangled groan and a laugh, but at least he started moving.

She clung to his shoulders, and it was all she could do to contain the intense waves of sensation and emotion that broke through her. It had been so long since they had last made love, since she had felt truly desired. She had never thought of herself as a particularly sensual person, but when she was with Tobias she felt acutely sensitive and, somehow, more alive. Pleasure zinged through her and, when he touched her, she practically purred. And, until this very moment, she hadn't realized how much she had *missed* Tobias despite the hurt, despite everything she had done to surgically remove him from her life.

Tobias found her mouth and kissed her then, suddenly, there was no containing anything as heat coiled and built unbearably, then splintered into the night.

Long minutes later, her eyes flipped open. She thought she had closed her eyes for just a few minutes, but in that time the phone lights had died, so she guessed it must have been an hour or more.

Outside, the wind was now gusting, and a light rain was still pattering on the windows, which meant the weather was blowing in off the sea. The air temperature had dropped, but she was toasty warm because Tobias's arm was wrapped around her waist, as if he wanted to keep her close, even in sleep.

Turning her head on the pillow, she tried to see his face, but it was now so dark, she couldn't make out actual features, so she consoled herself by snuggling in a bit closer. Although it was hard to relax, because she had loved making love with him, more than she could have imagined, and she wanted to do it again. And, now that she was awake, she didn't feel one bit tired.

The rain stopped, and there must have been a break in the clouds, because the room lightened. Propping herself on one elbow, Allegra stared at Tobias. Moonlight shafted more strongly through the French doors, illuminating his clean-cut profile and rock-solid jaw, the inky crescent of his lashes.

She had an almost overwhelming urge to reach out and trace the line of his jaw, wake him up and kiss him. Anticipation was already humming through her at the prospect of being in his arms again, but that gave her pause.

The giddy happiness welling up inside, the desire to throw caution to the winds and live in the moment, made her go still inside.

What if this was just an attraction that was finally

working its way toward a dead end and, after the month was up, they would both be over each other?

Or, maybe, just maybe, it was the real thing.

Her heart beat a little faster at the thought of settling down with Tobias, of a real relationship, maybe even marriage.

But she couldn't forget that the last time she had imagined a future with Tobias, he had ditched her.

That meant she had to start thinking, and not just feeling. Tobias was a challenge: used to command, and with a quiet, seasoned toughness that she knew stemmed from his years in Special Forces. And she couldn't forget that there had been no words of commitment, or love. Just the off-the-register attraction that had bound them together for six years.

As much as she wanted to reach out and touch him, to snuggle in close and rouse him with a kiss, she was suddenly certain that if she wanted to win Tobias, she would not do so by giving in and having sex with him again.

They had already made love, and nothing had changed.

Tobias had finally opened up about Lindsay, but getting information out of him had been like getting blood out of a stone. And the fact that he had left his fiancée because he had wanted her still niggled. Something about his confession just hadn't added up…then it finally came clear.

If Tobias had been fighting an attraction to Allegra for years, why had he gotten engaged to Lindsay in the first place? And why *stay* engaged, when he knew that he wanted someone else?

Then there was the fact that, when he had finally broken things off, he had not tried to start a relationship with her. He had just spent one night with her and walked away.

As if he didn't consider her relationship material.

As if he saw her the way some guys at university had, as some kind of clichéd beauty queen, who was only good for a casual fling. And, suddenly, a whole lot of other things fell into place.

They had been at each other's throats at the lawyers. Then, suddenly, he had wanted sex with her in the parking garage. Almost as if he had decided that, since she was in his house for the month, why not have sex with her, *and get her out of his system*?

The more she thought about it, the surer she became.

She was certain that if she did continue to have sex with Tobias, which would be the easy option, he would be only too happy, because it would confirm the image he had of her and make it easy to walk away at the end of the month.

And just like that, she was *back*.

Now, hopping mad, she moved carefully, so she wouldn't wake Tobias, who she no longer wanted to touch, and slipped from the bed. Her bare feet landed on cool, marble-smooth floorboards. She straightened, becoming aware of the faint stiffness that went with making love when she was unaccustomed to doing so, a stiffness she had only ever experienced once before.

That small fact made her even madder. The fact that she had only ever made love with Tobias was... worrying.

Since she liked it so much, why hadn't she slept with anyone else?

Tiptoeing around the room, she found her phone, picked up her clothes and sneakers, then went to the bathroom to freshen up and change.

As she zipped up her dress and pulled on her sneakers, she noted that one of her key problems was that she'd never had a casual approach to sex, because that just wasn't how she was wired. For starters, she was naturally suspicious of intimacy; she just didn't like people close when she didn't know them very well. And, after the "problem" in San Francisco, she had gotten even more hard line.

And yet, she had made love with Tobias, and made herself vulnerable to him in ways that he hadn't seemed to notice.

For a start, she had been a virgin.

Another thought occurred to her. Tobias had made a point of letting her know how important his engagement to Lindsay had been. Apparently, his attraction to Allegra had been a betrayal that Lindsay had not been able to forgive. But Tobias had not at any point asked her about her own engagement to Mike.

Her brows jerked together. She wondered how Tobias could not care that they were both, supposedly, betraying Mike in an even worse way?

Of course, the engagement wasn't real, but he didn't know that.

She briefly considered that Tobias had gotten swept away by passion and had simply forgotten she was engaged.

Or maybe he hadn't forgotten the engagement at all, *but saw making love to her as a legitimate way to cut Mike out and claim her for himself.*

She drew a slow breath as she examined the possibility. Tobias behaving that way made a curious kind of sense. His actions had not been above board or even honorable.

What they had been was *alpha*.

Ten

Allegra tiptoed downstairs, wincing when a floor-board creaked beneath her bare feet. When she reached the kitchen, she grabbed the jewelry box from the counter and let herself out the door onto the deck. Minutes later, sneakers on her feet, she was walking along the moonlit path back to the main house. At the top of the hill, the brightly lit windows of the mansion were like a warm beacon.

She checked her watch. It felt like hours had passed, but it wasn't quite midnight. She had only been in the beach house for just over three hours. Having some of the best sex of her life, and for only the second time in her life, *with the same man.*

As she climbed onto the terrace, she paused for a moment to take in the view, which was breathtaking.

The sky was filled with ragged clouds. Despite that, the moon was full and had turned the sea to molten silver, and etched the sweep of lawn with the jagged silhouettes of trees and the pitched roofline of the beach house.

She had left the fascinating painting of Alexandra behind, but she would retrieve that tomorrow. The main thing was that she had the jewelry, and she couldn't wait to get to her room so she could clean up the ring she had discovered and see if she could use it as a fake engagement ring.

Anxious to reach the sanctuary of her bedroom before Tobias caught up with her, she stepped inside and hurried through the dark corridor and up the stairs. She was well aware that she did not have a good track record with Tobias. If he caught up with her now, she would probably not be able to resist him. They would make love again, and that could be fatal.

In order to reverse the mistakes she'd made, she needed to move forward with the relationship strategy she had already put in place, otherwise what they had might stall and die. That meant no sex until Tobias was ready to use words like *love* and *commitment*.

She continued up the sweeping elegant stairs. Once inside her room, she closed the door, set the jewelry box down on her bedside table and flicked on the bedside lamp. She also remembered to put her phone on charge, since using the flashlight had drained the battery.

Shivering slightly, because the rainy weather had

definitely dropped the temperature, she drew the curtains.

She found fresh underwear, and the soft T-shirt and cotton shorts she liked to sleep in, and walked through to the bathroom. After quickly showering and washing her hair, because she wanted to leave super early in the morning before Tobias got up, she toweled herself dry. Once she was cozily belted into a light cotton bathrobe, she strapped her watch onto her wrist. That had gotten to be a habit, because she still liked to keep an eye on her heart rate. She then stood in front of the mirror as she combed out her hair and dried it.

As she did so, her gaze was drawn to a red mark on her neck, and another on her jawline. Small abrasions that were probably caused by the five-o'clock shadow on Tobias's jaw.

She drew a swift breath as heated memories surfaced. Tobias kissing her neck, nuzzling her jaw, biting down delicately on one lobe…

A soft click made her start. The sound had come from downstairs and was probably a door closing, which meant Tobias had walked back to the house. Instantly, her heart sped up.

She quickly switched off the bathroom light, then walked through to her bedroom and killed the bedside lamp, plunging the room into darkness. Maybe she was overreacting, but if Tobias knocked on her door, she didn't trust herself not to let him in. If he saw that her lights were off, chances were he would just go straight to bed.

Long seconds later, she heard his footsteps as he walked past her room, then the sound of his door closing.

Contrarily, she felt annoyed that he hadn't even so much as paused at her door. Feeling her way in the dark, she found her bed and sat down, keeping an eye on her watch, which glowed in the dark. A minute or so later, she heard the sound of a shower then, a few more minutes later, a door closing. When a further five minutes had passed without any sound, she flicked her lamp back on.

Hefting the jewelry box, she set it down on the bed. It looked even richer and more beautiful in the soft glow of the lamp. After she had removed the diary and set it down on the bedside table, she began emptying the velvet bags onto the white coverlet.

White wasn't the best background color to view the jewelry, and she wasn't a jeweler, so she couldn't be sure—maybe they were just paste—but the "diamond" jewelry looked breathtakingly real. She picked up the ring, which stood out as being different from the other pieces because it was smaller and plainer. With its cushion-shaped diamond and simple gold band, it was quite definitely an engagement ring.

Feeling almost as if she was trespassing on someone else's memories, she slipped the diamond ring onto her ring finger. It was too tight, which was a shame, but it looked pretty. She would have to get it resized before she could wear it.

Slipping the ring off, she returned it to its velvet bag. She then collected up all of the other jewels, placed them back into their velvet bags, then stowed them all in a zipped pocket in her handbag. She would take them into her favorite jeweler, Ambrosi, first thing in the morning. Hopefully, they would be able to assess the "diamonds" for her and resize the ring. Luckily, Ambrosi was in the Atraeus Mall, where she had arranged to meet Mike for their "getting the ring date," so that would save her some time.

She put the antique jewelry box away in the walk-in closet, then checked her phone, which was now showing some charge. She texted Mike, to give him a heads-up to check the schedule she had given him, because he needed to meet her at the Atraeus Mall tomorrow at twelve p.m. sharp.

Dragging back the coverlet, she climbed into bed and switched the lamp out, but just as she was finally sliding into sleep, inspiration struck, and she sat bolt upright in bed.

Eighteen months ago, a girlfriend had treated her to an online seminar called *How to Get Your Alpha Man*. It had been run by Elena Lyons-Messena, who was a psychologist and something of a spa guru.

Pulled from Elena's own personal experience, it had been blunt and to the point. You didn't get your alpha man, who was a natural leader of the pack, by being soft and doing whatever he wanted you to do.

You got him by taking charge, by being opinionated and even difficult, because alpha men liked a challenge. If they thought you were just going to sleep with them and be all soft and cute, you could kiss the relationship goodbye, because they would be doing what alpha men did, looking for the next challenge.

From memory, there had been two key tactics, both based around availability.

Firstly, you had to make it clear that you would not always be available to him, but that you would fit him in when you could.

Secondly, make it clear that your schedule included *other men*. Once an alpha knew that you were available to other men, and that those men found you intensely desirable, it was a game changer.

Elena had been firm on the point that the strategy worked, because it catered to the alpha's natural instincts to fight for the woman they wanted, and to win her. As ruthless as the tactics were, she had suggested that the strategies could actually be viewed as a form of kindness toward your alpha male, because you got him through the whole pursuit-and-choice thing quickly, and then everyone could relax.

She had also noted that, if none of the strategies worked, you needed to save yourself and leave him. At this point, the best-case scenario was that the alpha would wake up to what he had lost, come after you, and propose. Worst-case scenario: you would discover that you had gotten it completely wrong, and you could then get on with the rest of your life.

Now, thoroughly awake, Allegra flicked on her bedside lamp and found the book that went with the workshop. She flipped to the chapter on commitment. The first paragraphs seemed to leap off the page.

Warning: Sleeping with an alpha before they have committed is risky, because they can view the sex as "the prize," and you could end up being the victim of a one-night stand. If you have slept with your alpha too soon, you need to quickly find a way to reject him.

With alphas, "no" is a good word.

Shades of her mom!

According to the book, she had already committed the cardinal sin with Tobias, *twice*.

She had given him the prize of sex, and he hadn't had to pursue her to attain it, because both times she had practically seduced him. If there was a hunter in their "relationship," it was her.

That had to change.

She didn't know what the result of tonight's lovemaking would be but, given their track record, and the fact that Tobias was meeting Francesca some time tomorrow, she did not think Tobias had commitment in mind.

If she still wanted Tobias, that meant *she* had to change the way she behaved right now.

Uncannily, she had already made a start on Elena's strategy by trying, to make herself "unavailable" to Tobias, and signaling that she was available to another man, by getting "engaged" to Mike.

She was taking a risk by continuing with the charade, but the way she saw it, she had no choice.

She could not commit herself to a man who might

never reach the point of committing to her. If Tobias didn't fight for her, it was a no-brainer. She needed to follow Elena's advice and walk away from a relationship that had already consumed six years of her life.

Just the thought of playing that kind of game made her heart beat faster, because a part of her just wanted to cling to Tobias and build on what they had.

But that would only result in her getting ditched again.

Eleven

The sun was attempting to diffuse a dawn glow through sullen, dense clouds as Allegra dressed in a gorgeous, short turquoise skirt with a matching cam-isole top, and a sheer white blouse that went over top. The gauzy blouse tied in a knot at hip-level, giving the whole outfit a sharp, but groovy, holiday vibe. As a final touch, she secured the Chanel earrings through her lobes, then slipped into a pair of strappy turquoise heels. She checked her watch, noting that it was almost seven, a whole hour earlier than she nor-mally left for work, and shoveled her purse, makeup and phone into a white tote.

Her hair was still loose, and she hadn't put on any makeup, but she would do all of that when she got to work. Her main concern was to get out of the house before Tobias got up because, at a guess, he was going to be annoyed that she had walked out on him last night, and would want to know why. That was a conversation she didn't want to have right now.

The way she saw it, it was imperative that she move forward with her "engagement" to Mike, and it was entirely possible that Tobias, being the alpha that he was, would demand that she get rid of Mike while she was sleeping with him.

If Tobias was masterful enough, and gave her that look that made her knees melt, she could not guarantee that she wouldn't weaken and agree to "give up" Mike. If she did that, she would be throwing away the only leverage she had.

She didn't know how long she would be able to keep up the charade. At an optimistic best guess, she had a day, because by tonight Tobias would be totally ticked off and, if all went according to plan, he would demand a conversation.

At that point, he would realize the danger: that he was about to lose her to another man and, hopefully, would be galvanized to fight to win her back.

So, first off, she needed to get out of the house without Tobias seeing her. Second, she needed to move forward with making her "engagement" to Mike look more convincing than it currently did. Her plan was to take a nice pic of them having a romantic champagne lunch together to use as a screen saver on her phone. Tobias would then see it, because she would casually place her phone near him. Third, she would wait for Tobias to initiate a conversation about how he couldn't bear for her to marry Mike, because he had realized he couldn't live without her.

Before she left her room, she did a quick check of the jewelry, frowning when she noted that one of the old velvet bags had actually split open. Rummaging in her drawers, she found a portable jewelry case, emptied out the pretty selection of costume jewelry and dropped that in her tote. Once the jewelry had been assessed, she would toss the shabby old velvet bags and store the pieces in the case.

She grabbed a light rain jacket and tossed it over one arm. Apparently, there was some kind of storm system heading their way, so the weather was going to get worse, not better. After a last check of her appearance, she walked to the door and paused to listen. When all seemed quiet, she turned the ornate brass knob but, a split second before she opened the door, she heard the sound of footsteps and the low tones of Tobias's voice, as if he was talking on his phone.

Her heart slammed against her chest. Tobias was already up. She drew a deep breath and waited long seconds, just in case he was about to walk down to the kitchen. When she didn't hear anything further, she opened the door a crack. She could hear his voice in the distance, so he was obviously still on a call, but the hall was empty.

Breathing a sigh of relief, she stepped out into the hall and gently closed her door behind her. She made her way downstairs and cut through the kitchen, which were closest to the garage. When she reached her car, she delved into her tote in search of her keys. When she didn't find them, her stomach sank.

With all the turmoil of moving into Tobias's house, *and the kiss in her room yesterday afternoon*, she hadn't returned the keys to her handbag as she usually would. She had a vague recollection of setting them down on one of the bedside tables. That meant that when she had transferred items from one handbag to another this morning, she had not stowed her car keys, because they were still on her bedside table.

Dropping her tote and the rain jacket in the passenger seat, she jogged to the kitchen, then started up the grand, curving staircase, listening intently as she went.

Her pulse pounded when she heard a door pop open. She froze. Luckily, she was just far enough around the curve of the staircase that she wasn't visible to anyone in the hall. Although, if Tobias was walking toward the stairs, she was busted.

A few seconds later, she heard the click of a door closing. Straightening, she walked as quickly and quietly as she could to her room, ducked inside and found the keys.

She was tempted to brazenly stroll out of her door and down the stairs, but an innate caution made her pause. The sound of footsteps in the hall confirmed her decision. She waited for Tobias to walk past her door. He was clearly on his way to the kitchen so, once he was safely there, she could sneak down the stairs and leave via the front door.

His footsteps slowed, then stopped directly outside her door. She froze, certain he was about to knock. A split second later, she heard an audible vibration, then Tobias's low, curt tones as he answered a phone call. His voice receded, signaling that he was walking away as he took the call.

She made herself wait one more minute, then quietly opened the door and stepped out into the hall. Taking a deep breath, she walked as quietly as she could down the stairs, checked that Tobias was nowhere in sight, then tiptoed across the grand front foyer. Moments later, she was outside and walking around the side of the house to the garage. Luckily, none of the kitchen windows overlooked the garage, so she should be free and clear.

Tobias strolled through to the study to collect his briefcase, which, in all the confusion of moving in yesterday afternoon, he had left there.

He kept his phone to his ear as Tulley, the private investigator he had tasked to check out both Allegra and Mike, ran through a dry list of facts about Allegra. Facts that he already knew and that provided details of the scandal that had unfolded in San Francisco, but which did nothing to further illuminate what had happened.

Tobias had hoped Tulley might find evidence of coercion or financial pressure that would explain what his gut told him didn't fit, because the more time he spent with Allegra, the more discordant the online stories seemed.

And, after the couple of hours they had spent together in the beach house last night, he had been forcibly struck by something he should have seen before. Allegra was gorgeous, confident and mouth-wateringly sexy, but she was also ultra-organized, assertive and direct.

Those qualities didn't sit easily with claims made by social media sites that she was an ambitious party girl using her looks and sex to snag a wealthy husband. Added to that, Tobias had found that, when it came to sex, if anything, Allegra was slightly awkward, even a little shy, almost as if she was unaccustomed to intimacy.

He frowned as that thought brought back a memory of the first time they had made love, two years ago. At the time, as unlikely as it had seemed, it had passed through his mind that Allegra could have been a virgin. But then he had read the online scandal around her and decided there was no way. Then Lindsay had miscarried, and he had done the only thing he decently could, and broken with Allegra completely.

His jaw tightened as a hot flash of the way Allegra had pressed against him last night sent a wave of heat through him. If she was not the free-and-easy party girl that certain social media accounts made her out to be, but the focused-and-professional businesswoman she appeared to be in Miami, then that made sense of her walking out on him last night.

From her point of view, his behavior had been self-centered and insensitive *for the second time*.

As he picked up the briefcase, a flash of movement caught his eye. He glanced up in time to see Allegra, in a short turquoise skirt and a filmy white blouse and wearing high heels, jog across the gravel drive in the direction of the garage.

Dropping the briefcase back on the couch, he curtly told Tulley he would call him back. Terminating the call, he strode toward the kitchen. The throaty purr of her convertible starting broke the morning silence as he went through the door that opened onto a covered walk. Two strides later, he stepped into the garage.

Allegra was in the process of backing out. He called her name and was almost certain her gaze locked with his as she braked. Although, it was difficult to tell, because she was wearing sunglasses. A split second later, she spun the wheel and disappeared down the drive.

Jaw taut, he found her number and rang her. The call went straight through to voice mail.

He left a brief message, then slid his phone back in his pocket.

There was definitely a problem. He didn't know what, yet, but he would find out.

As far as he knew, Allegra never went anywhere without her phone. She was either on it, or she was listening to music, but there was no way she didn't know he was calling her. She just hadn't chosen to answer.

His jaw tightened as he returned to the sitting room and hit redial on Tulley's number.

It occurred to him that he had been asking the wrong questions.

Online social media platforms were notorious for twisted stories and outright lies. He had been the victim of a few himself. Four months ago, social media influencer, Buffy Hamilton, had, entirely by chance, been snapped with him at the same charity event. She had then implied they had spent the night together. JT had been on his case for weeks.

When Tulley picked up the call, Tobias told him to email him a copy of the report, then tasked him to do a second investigation, this time on the two wealthy guys, Fischer and Halliday, who had claimed that Allegra had slept with them for expensive gifts, and to further her career.

"I want to know everything," he said curtly. "And I want the report yesterday."

"Uh…before you hang up, I think you might want to hear what I found out about Mike Callaghan."

Tobias frowned. He had almost forgotten about Callaghan. "Go ahead."

"Aside from being employed by Miss Mallory as a yoga instructor and personal trainer, the guy's an actor. Apparently, he's waiting to see if he's got a part in some online-streaming daytime soap based in Hollywood, and once he's got that, he's out of here. And, get this…he's got a girlfriend. That is, someone other than Miss Mallory. And, apparently, he and Miss Mallory don't seem to have ever dated. In fact, my source, who works with them both, didn't even know they were a couple. Furthermore, she was pretty sure Miss Mallory was over Callaghan as an employee, and was on the verge of firing him."

Until she found a further use for him.

Satisfaction relaxed the tension that had gripped Tobias ever since Allegra had announced that she was engaged.

It was official. The engagement was fake.

In all likelihood, she had chosen Callaghan for the role *because* he was an actor. If that was the case, she had to be paying him. Given that her finances were stretched with starting a new business, and that she was looking to expand, that was something she probably couldn't afford.

The only reason that made sense of the fake engagement was that Allegra wanted to make it clear she'd had nothing to do with the clause in Esmae's will.

But then she had given him the exact opposite message by sleeping with him.

Tobias pinched the bridge of his nose. He couldn't believe it, but he was actually beginning to lose track of what was happening. It was a far cry from his days in tactical military intelligence when he had used to track down terrorist cells. But those were days when one plus one equaled two. And, with Allegra, apparently, that equation could add up to almost any number, depending on what she wanted. If she had been a spy, she would have run circles around the CIA, the KGB, Mossad…hell, everyone.

A little grimly, he noted that it was time to step away from a situation that was getting more and more entangled by the day. The only problem was, after last night, he didn't want to step away.

He wanted her back.

The decision settled in. There was no logic to the decision, just pure, unadulterated desire. Despite the red flags, he found Allegra to be quirky, challenging and fascinating. Making love with her was nothing short of addictive. After years of what had devolved into something less than a friendship with Lindsay, followed by the superficial relationships that had filled the gap since then, keeping Allegra in his bed was a no-brainer.

Fake engagement or not, he didn't want out.

And, if Allegra thought she could walk away from him without at least an explanation, she could think again.

He found the dating schedule he had picked up off the driveway yesterday and unfolded it. Two years ago, he had left Allegra cold. Now, he had to consider that he had made a mistake. He had hurt her, but he would make it up to her, if she would let him. But, first, they needed a conversation, and that was going to happen at... He found the date with Callaghan, which was scheduled for today, at the Atraeus Mall. At twelve, sharp.

Tulley cleared his throat. "Do you still want me to, uh...keep an eye on Miss Mallory?"

A flash of Allegra jogging across the drive, clearly

trying to avoid him, played through his mind. She was up to something. His jaw tightened. Hell, yes.

In a clipped voice, he gave Tulley his orders. Keep an eye on Allegra's movements for the morning. "If she and Callaghan leave the resort together, call me."

Terminating the call, he walked through to the kitchen to make coffee. As far as Tobias was concerned, now that he and Allegra had made love, Callaghan should be out of the picture, but there were no indicators that that was happening.

He found grounds and started the filter machine. He should have made sure Callaghan was gone last night. The only problem was, he hadn't been exactly interested in conversation until he had woken up to find Allegra gone.

He had walked up to the house and noted that Allegra's light was on but, by the time he had reached the door of her room, her light was out.

He had considered knocking. Maybe it was just a coincidence that her light had gone out just seconds before he had gotten there, but he didn't think so. She had been avoiding him.

That notion had been confirmed just minutes ago when he had watched her accelerating down the drive.

Frowning, he went over the sequence of events that had led to their lovemaking, then the encounter itself. From memory, there hadn't been a lot of conversation. In point of fact, his interactions with Allegra were the exact opposite of those he had with every other date he could remember.

But then, what he felt for Allegra was a whole lot different to what he'd felt for any other woman. It was a fact that his feelings were knee-jerk and intense and, he had to admit, his manners were mostly absent.

Normally, he was methodical and controlled in most areas of his life—in business, and especially in relationships. One of Lindsay's criticisms of him had been that he had been too locked down, too reserved. But, when it came to Allegra, he could not even seem to control his responses.

The rich fragrance of coffee filled the kitchen. Tobias filled a mug, but, before drinking it, he spread the two-page dating schedule out on the counter.

The crisp organization inherent in every neatly formed box was impressive. It confirmed that Allegra was take-charge and detail-oriented, even when it came to her personal life, and that, evidently, Callaghan did take orders.

Despite his frustration over Allegra neatly avoiding him last night, and this morning, he grinned at the thought. Even if he hadn't known Callaghan was a fake, the way she ran him around was clear evidence that he was all wrong for her. She would be bored with him in ten seconds flat.

Tobias studied Allegra's bolded instruction that she would organize a ring. The word was clearly code for the fact that Allegra would be providing the ring.

His jaw compressed at the thought that she was going to the expense of buying a ring when she couldn't afford to do so.

On impulse, he retrieved his phone and opened up the email with the attachment of the report Tulley had just sent through.

He had never thought overlong about Allegra as a businesswoman—he had been too busy focusing on nixing the attraction that sizzled between them—but now that aspect of her was brought sharply into view.

He knew she had a business degree from Stanford, but Tulley had clarified that it was actually a master's in Finance, which was a considerably more prestigious, longer and more difficult degree. To add to the picture, apparently she had been a driven student, because she had graduated with distinction, with a grade point average of 4.7, which was crazy good.

Suddenly, the picture of Allegra as a good-time girl in search of a wealthy husband didn't even come close to panning out.

If that was her goal, and with her looks, she could have married at eighteen and spent her life shopping and lunching. Instead, she had gotten into Stanford, which was no easy task. Then, she had worked for five years for a degree that fitted her out for a high-flying career in the financial fast lane, earning six figures just to start.

One of the top West Coast financial firms, Burns-Stein Halliday, had recruited her. Just months later, her reputation in shreds, she had walked away from the firm and her career.

Almost six years of hard work and focused ambition gone, because she had, apparently, decided that sex was a priority.

He set his coffee down, suddenly annoyed. He didn't think so.

To the best of his knowledge, Allegra had seldom dated at all. If she had one obsession, it was her business. And, in the two years she had been living in Miami, he only knew of one guy she had slept with, and that was him.

For the first time, he seriously considered that Allegra had been set up.

Tulley had made brief notes about the two men with whom she was supposed to have had wild extramarital affairs. They were both connected with the firm, one an executive who was married to the senior partner's daughter, the other an executive who was the nephew of one of the other partners. That instantly raised a red flag.

Why would Allegra risk sleeping with either of them, when she had to have known it could cost her the career for which she had worked so hard?

Tulley had included pictures of the two men. They were both now in their forties and fifties with the typical lean, tanned look of players. One of them even sported a diamond stud in one lobe. Neither of them was married now, but they both had been when the alleged scandal had happened.

He sat back in his chair. Adrenaline was running through his veins. He was beginning to feel the way he had before he had gone on a mission, coldly focused, ticked off and on edge.

If it turned out that one, or both, of those men had lied, probably to protect their own reputations in business, he would make it his business to expose what they had done.

And, if they had cost Allegra her career, they could pay for it.

Pushing to his feet, he finished his coffee, rinsed the cup and put it in the dishwasher.

Retrieving his briefcase, he walked through to the garage. With any luck, since he would be at the Ocean Beach Resort today, moving in as manager, he might even run into Allegra.

But, he wasn't betting on that happening.

Which was why he would make it a priority to be at the Atraeus Mall when she was supposed to be meeting with Callaghan.

Placing his briefcase on the passenger-side seat, he swung behind the wheel. But before he started the truck, he made a call to JT, who had connections in Hollywood, and instructed him to offer a large cash contribution to the production Callaghan had auditioned for, on the condition that they hired him *today*.

Forty minutes later, en route from his Hunt Security office to the Ocean Beach Resort, he took a call from JT. Callaghan had verbally accepted the contract offer.

Satisfaction eased some of the tension that gripped him.

When it came to Allegra, he was fiercely, uncompromisingly possessive. He'd spent six years trying to deny the attraction, because he just hadn't seen her as relationship material. She was almost too gorgeous and terminally high maintenance, with a stream of guys constantly vying for her attention. Then, when Lindsay had miscarried, the guilt that had hit him had underlined that giving in to temptation where Allegra was concerned had been a serious mistake.

But, two years on, he was beginning to realize that he had misread Allegra, and how much he *liked* her: the sass and the challenge, her sharp business mind and fierce independence; the fact that she ran rings around most men, including him. And the more he uncovered about the *real* Allegra, the more strongly he was attracted to her.

The plain fact was, he didn't just want her in his bed; he was beginning to want a whole lot more than that.

The thought of Callaghan placing an engagement ring on Allegra's finger, even as a sham, made his jaw lock.

That would happen over his dead body.

Twelve

Allegra drove into the underground parking garage of the Atraeus mall at eleven thirty, which would give her plenty of time to pick up the ring from the jeweler's before Mike arrived.

Hooking the strap of her tote over her shoulder, she took the elevator up to the ground floor and stepped out into the fabulous foyer, with its marble floors and glittering high-end boutiques.

Because she had wanted to avoid Tobias until she had the ring on her finger, she had deliberately absented herself from the spa. As it happened, she had put her time to good use, with meetings with her banker, then the real estate agent who had listed the property she was hoping would be her new spa. Now, all she needed was for Mike to turn up at twelve, as instructed.

She glanced around the mall, just in case Mike was early. He wasn't, so she decided to use the time to get a bunch of roses from the florist. The plan was simple. Buy the flowers, get the ring and install it on her finger, then snap some pics of herself looking vibrant and happy with Mike looking like a handsome, devoted fiancé. When that was done, she would install the pic as a screen saver and go back to the resort.

The heady scent of flowers wafted around her as she walked past buckets of cut blooms and beautiful bunches of roses. Automatically, she chose a dozen red roses, because they shouted romance *and* they would look totally striking against the turquoise and white of her outfit. She paid for them and strolled back out into the mall. As she did so, she glimpsed a tall, dark guy in a suit as he disappeared into an elevator. She stopped dead, her heart pounding, because she had been almost certain that was Tobias, although it couldn't be. She knew for a fact that he was spending the day at the resort with Marc, because she had checked.

She had a sudden flash of the annoyance on Tobias's face as she had backed out of the garage. Happily, she had thought to put her sunglasses on, so she had been able to pretend that she hadn't noticed him.

When she decided she had space in her day for him, he would see the ring and the flowers and understand that, just because they had slept together, that didn't mean she was happy to fall in with his plans to have casual, uncommitted sex with her for the next month.

She checked her watch and studied the bustling traffic, which was predominantly female. Mike was tall and distinctive; he would be easy to spot. Her gaze snagged on a small guy with blond hair who was standing, quite still, amid the milling shoppers, a phone in his hand, and who, at that moment, just happened to be looking directly at her.

It was a little creepy, but she instantly dismissed him as a husband who had been abandoned in the mall, and who was probably waiting for his wife to emerge from a boutique.

Juggling the flowers, Allegra extracted her phone from her tote and checked to see if Mike had texted or called. He hadn't. She tapped his number and waited while it rang. When he didn't pick up, she left a voice message.

She decided there was no point hanging around waiting for him, so she strolled toward Ambrosi, a fabulous designer jeweler that had started out life as a pearl house on the Mediterranean island of Medinos. Ordinarily, she would be excited to just walk through those doors and breathe in the romance of a store that had started out life in antiquity and was gorgeously decorated to reflect that past. But, after last night, romance was off her list. Today was all about getting on track with her new agenda, which was to drive Tobias crazy with jealousy.

To that end, first thing that morning she had

brought the ring in to be resized, and the other jewelry to be cleaned and assessed. The sales clerk had promised they would be ready by twelve.

As she strolled toward the glass doors, her reflection bounced back at her. With her hair piled up in a messy knot, the red roses against her white shirt, and the vivid turquoise mini and high heels, she definitely looked sharp. Just as she was about to step through the doors, she glimpsed the little man who had been looking at her before, directly behind her. This time his phone was up, and he was definitely taking a photo.

Her jaw tightened. Before she had left San Francisco, a guy who had probably been inspired by the lies posted about her, had used to follow her around, take pictures and share them online. She had put the cops onto him, and he had been stopped. Since then, she had developed a zero tolerance for being stalked. If this creep was still hanging around when she left the store, she would take *his* picture and let him know that, if she ever saw him again, it would be sent to the police.

The store assistant, a young, beautifully groomed woman called Fleur, produced the ring, which now sparkled with an eye-catching brilliance. "Just wait one moment, and I'll get the other jewelry you brought in. I think Clark has almost finished buffing it."

Allegra set the bunch of roses down and picked the ring up off the black velvet pad the store assistant had placed it on. She slid the ring onto the third finger of her left hand, but, as she did so, her mood, which had been upbeat, bottomed out and a curious sense of disappointment assailed her. She had been so busy with her plans to ramp up the fake engagement, she hadn't thought about how wearing the ring would make her feel.

Brought up with parents who had been in love and totally devoted to each other, she had always imagined that she was destined to experience the same kind of nurturing, protective love. That, when an engagement ring went onto her finger, it would be an emotionally loaded moment, shared with a man who would swear to love and honor her. That the ring on her finger would symbolize the beginning of their shared life of love and intimacy.

Instead, she had a fake engagement, a fake ring, a fake fiancé who would probably not even keep the appointment she had paid him to keep and a stubbornly addictive attraction to a man who only wanted her for sex.

Swallowing against a sudden tightness in her throat, she wrenched the ring off. As she did so, Fleur returned with a tall, gaunt man in a pristine suit, who looked more like an undertaker than a jeweler.

He placed the shabby pile of black velvet bags down on one side of the counter, then set down a large, signature Ambrosi box. He flicked the lid open with a flourish and extracted the necklace. A quick glance at Fleur and she scurried to produce a black velvet pad. With solemn, reverential movements, he arranged the necklace, which had developed a fiery glow beneath the dazzling LED lights.

Allegra's breath caught, despite knowing that the necklace, like most of the other jewelry, had to be fakes. Why else would Esmae, who had loved wearing the Hunt diamonds, have shoved them in a box in a dusty attic?

Clark produced an envelope and extracted two sheets of paper, which he spread out on the counter. "I've done a quick assessment, but if you like I can get you a more detailed second opinion from someone who deals in antique jewelry for insurance purposes—"

"What do you mean, insurance purposes?"

Clark gave her a transfixed look. "You don't have either the Faberge diamond necklace and earrings, or the Van Cleef and Arpels bracelet and brooch, insured?"

Feeling distinctly shell-shocked, Allegra walked out of Ambrosi with the roses and a small fortune in diamonds in her tote: rare, designer diamonds with the kind of provenance that would guarantee sky-high values. Jewelry that Esmae had never mentioned, and that Allegra's own family knew nothing about.

Because she knew so little about the jewelry, she wasn't prepared to call any of it hers. They could be Hunt jewels, perhaps belonging to Tobias's natural grandmother. Although, if that was the case, why had Esmae possessed them? And why had she kept such fabulously expensive jewels separate from the Hunt diamonds, which were cataloged and stored in a bank vault?

The other thought that had occurred, and which was much more likely, was that they were some kind of second Mallory skeleton in their scandal-ridden closet; that they had been hidden because they were *stolen*.

Either way, before she did anything with them, *and ended up in prison*, she needed to know more. She needed to read Alexandra's journal.

Lost in thought, Allegra made a beeline for the restaurant where she and Mike were supposed to have their engagement date. As she strolled, she checked her phone again. Mike hadn't acknowledged her text, and he still hadn't made any attempt to call her.

Keeping the phone in her hand on the off chance that he would actually call, she lengthened her stride. The café was just around the next corner. A split second later, just ahead, a familiar set of broad shoulders and the back of a well-shaped head registered.

Tobias.

He was casually striding, his phone held to one ear.

So, it had been him she had seen earlier. Shocked that he should turn up here, now, she spun on her heel and walked briskly back toward the main foyer. Mike wasn't here, so why go to the café at all? The last thing she needed right now was to have to deal with Tobias.

Stepping past a beautifully dressed couple, she almost ran down the same little man she had seen taking her photo earlier. "You!"

Clearly, he wasn't used to being confronted, because he froze like a deer in the headlights.

Holding up her phone and almost dropping the roses, which she now wished she had never bought, she snapped his photo. "There's no point pretending you aren't following me," she said coolly. "Tell me your name, or I go straight to the police."

"His name's Tulley," a deep, curt voice said, from behind her. "He works for me."

Allegra spun, adrenaline pumping as her gaze clashed with Tobias's. "Doing what?"

Although she already knew. Tulley who seemed to have an unhealthy zeal for sneaking around spying on people, probably belonged to Tobias's overpriced detective agency.

"Tulley's a PI."

The confirmation that Tobias was having her watched, *investigated*, sent a searing dart of hurt through her. It meant that he hadn't believed a word she'd said about her innocence, that he didn't trust her, *and that he had slept with her anyway.*

But, if he thought she was going to crumble, he could think again. "At least spying is marginally better than stalking. But if you truly believe all of the lies that have been written about me online, then we're done."

Shoving her phone in her tote, she turned away, but Tobias stepped ahead, blocking her.

"I don't believe them," he said quietly. "Babe, the reason Tulley's been following you is because I wanted him to keep an eye on you until I could get here. We need to talk."

Her jaw tightened against her automatic delight that he had called her *babe,* and the utter relief that he had finally seen that she wasn't a shallow party girl those social media accounts had made her out to be. But the fact that he had sicced Tulley on her meant that, at some level, he still didn't trust her.

Deliberately, she checked her watch. "Will it take long?"

"I guess I deserved that." He was silent for a beat. "After you ran out on me this morning—"

"I didn't 'run out' on you. I drove to work."

His gaze, the icy-hot one that set her on edge and turned her on all at once, drilled into her for long moments. "After you *drove to work*, I asked Tulley to keep an eye on you because the hell I was going to let Callaghan near you before we could have the conversation we should have had last night."

Conversation? For a long drawn-out moment, it was difficult to absorb the heart-pounding possibility that Tobias might, finally, be falling for her. That her strategy had worked even faster than she could have imagined. "What conversation, exactly, would that be?"

"This, for a start." Tobias produced a folded-up document she instantly recognized as the dating schedule she had given to Mike the previous day.

"According to the schedule, you and Callaghan are getting a ring today."

Cheeks warming, she snatched the paper out of his hand. "That doesn't belong to you. Where did you get it from?"

"Callaghan dropped it on the drive yesterday."

That figured. As of that moment, Callaghan— *Mike*—was fired as her fiancé.

She dropped the crumpled schedule into her tote. "Last I heard, getting a ring is an entirely normal thing for an engaged couple to—"

"You can't be engaged to Callaghan," he said flatly. "Not when you're sleeping with me."

A heated surge of emotion practically welded her to the spot. Tobias's statement that she was sleeping with him, the narrowed, glittering glance, as if he was Tarzan and she was Jane, was unequivocal and possessive enough to send chills down her spine.

Tobias definitely wanted her.

She registered that Tobias's abrupt declaration— the alpha male equivalent of staking claim—was what she had wanted from him two years ago, and what she had absolutely needed from him last night.

It wasn't flowery; it did not contain the word *love*, or anything at all about emotion or commitment. It was irritable and bad-tempered, even dictatorial, but that was what made her heart sing, because it was evidence that Tobias felt something real for her and that, finally, he was prepared to fight for her.

Then, she registered the ultimatum. Because she had slept with Tobias last night, she couldn't be engaged to Callaghan—that is, *Mike*, she corrected herself, irritated that she was starting to think like Tobias. "You're hardly in a position to give me an ultimatum when you've made it crystal clear that *you're* not interested in a relationship."

"I am now."

Allegra stared at the visible pulse beating along the side of Tobias's jaw. Dimly, she was aware of a cluster of teenage girls drifting past, giving him interested looks, and that, at some point, Tulley had left. Dimly, she registered that the bustling sounds of the mall, the hum of conversations, seemed to have fallen away. For long seconds, it was as if they were enclosed in an intimate bubble, where only the two of them existed.

She met Tobias's gaze squarely. "I won't sleep with you just because it's convenient for the month."

"Convenient?" His brows jerked together. "Believe me, sleeping with you has nothing to do with *convenience*—"

Tobias's hand closed briefly around her upper arm as he moved her out of the path of a motorized wheelchair. In the process, the top of her head brushed against his jaw, one palm landed against the solid muscle of his chest, and she caught the heady scents of soap and clean skin and cologne.

His gaze locked on hers. "Damn, I wish we weren't—"

"Tobias!"

Allegra stiffened. Tobias frowned and let her go. Francesca Messena-Atraeus had just strolled out of the opulent jeweler they just happened to be standing next to and which was, ironically, Atraeus Jewels.

For a split second, Allegra was so shocked to see the beautiful fashion designer that she didn't notice what she was wearing. Then, the silky, turquoise mini and camisole top, the filmy white shirt and high, strappy turquoise heels registered.

Had she mentioned that her outfit was an ultra-expensive Messena design?

Her stomach sank. There were some moments that got impressed indelibly, and damagingly, on a person's psyche; she was pretty sure this was one of them, because there was a *rule* about women wearing the exact same outfit.

And it didn't stop there. Even their hair was done the same, *and* their nail color matched. They could have been a mirror image of each other, the only difference being that Allegra's hair color was darker than Francesca's, which was currently a tawny blond.

And, as Francesca strolled toward them, a truth she just hadn't seen hit her forcibly.

She had seen buying Francesca's line of clothing, handbags and shoes, as a sign that she had healed, that she didn't hold a grudge that Francesca had stolen her man, and that she had moved on. But now, she understood exactly what she had been doing. She had made herself over *as Francesca*, so that Tobias would fall for her.

The sick feeling in her stomach was a confirmation she didn't want, but which she needed to face.

Two years ago, her hair had been long, with luxurious waves. Now, it was still long, but layered, so that it swung sexily around her face, a virtual mirror image of Francesca's current cut.

She had also changed her normal low-key colors on her nails to flamboyant pinks and, instead of lower more comfortable shoes, she had begun wearing gorgeous high heels that were more about looks than practicality. Again, just like Francesca.

She had even bought a range of silk lingerie that Francesca had said was her favorite on one of her social media sites. The cost had been astronomical, and now she knew why she had splurged on something she would not normally have bought.

Another horrifying thought struck. She had to wonder if the reason Tobias had showed a renewed interest in her was that she looked a whole lot more like Francesca than she had two years ago? That the reason he had made love to her was that he saw her as some kind of Francesca substitute?

Her mother had been right, she thought blankly. Somehow, she had allowed Tobias's rejection of her to affect her at a deep, bedrock level, to the point that she had even lost confidence in her own attractiveness.

But that wouldn't be happening any longer.

And, if Tobias thought that she was going to continue to be some kind of Barbie-doll substitute for the woman he couldn't have, he could think again.

Francesca jogged the last few yards, went up on her toes, wound her arms around Tobias's neck, hugged him close and kissed him on the cheek. But it was Tobias's reaction that commanded her attention. When his arms went around Francesca, he grinned, his teeth white against his tanned skin. Feeling increasingly miserable, she registered that he wasn't just attracted to Francesca, he *liked* her.

Francesca pulled free, but kept her arm around Tobias's waist, as she waved at a tall, blond friend who had just stepped out of a nearby boutique. She introduced the woman, whose name was Clara, to Tobias with the gleeful announcement that this was the gorgeous guy who was taking her out for dinner that night.

Allegra froze, for long seconds, stunned, then thoughts and emotions cascaded. She knew why Francesca was here; it was a business visit. But this didn't look or feel like business, *and Tobias was taking her out to dinner.*

She wished it didn't matter. But it did, because, for a few moments, she had thought that she and Tobias were finally on the brink of something special.

Now, the fact that Tobias had never taken her out for dinner, or even asked her for a coffee, struck deep. Just like he had never thought to buy her flowers or to give her any of the small gifts that were part of courtship.

She blinked, feeling like a sleeper just waking up. The way he was with Francesca suddenly seemed to point out all the lacks in their relationship, the huge abyss between what Tobias was offering and what she wanted.

And what she wanted wasn't so outrageous. They

were ordinary, everyday dreams that shouldn't be so hard to attain, like a man of her own, a home they could share and, sometime in the not-too-distant, misty future, babies to love. All of the things a lot of women of her acquaintance had already, and which they took for granted, but which had, so far, eluded Allegra.

The problem was, trying to be in a relationship with Tobias was like hitting a brick wall. All they shared was sex.

Despite trying to appear casual and unaffected, *as if meeting the other woman in Tobias's life barely impinged upon her*, Allegra's face felt frozen as introductions were made.

Happily, Francesca breezed past the fact that they were dressed like twins by complimenting Allegra on her great taste in clothing. Despite feeling embarrassed by the clothing issue, and deeply hurt at the way Tobias had failed to court her in any way, Allegra briefly acknowledged that, if Francesca wasn't after Tobias, they would probably be friends.

When Tobias mentioned Madison Spas, the transfixed look on Francesca's face gave Allegra the distinct impression that Francesca had suddenly placed her, and not in a good way. That meant she knew about the scandal in her past.

She didn't come across that reaction so often these days, especially not in the spa business, which was so far removed from her previous career it could be on another planet. But, every now and then, the past did jump out to bite her.

Allegra managed a polite, professional reply, then Francesca surprised her by asking specific questions about her spa treatments. Normally, she would be in her element talking about mud wraps and their super foods menu, but relaxing was difficult because every time Francesca touched Tobias's arm with a small, intimate gesture, she felt miserable and increasingly tense.

Because despite the hurt of the past, despite her strategy and the caution she had thought she was exercising, she had fallen for Tobias, hook, line and sinker.

Again.

Thirteen

Allegra's phone trilled. Relieved to have an excuse not to look at the gorgeous couple Francesca and Tobias made, she fished it out of her tote.

The call was from Mike. She had been so distracted that she had completely forgotten about him. "Where are you?"

"Uh… MIA."

Her brows jerked together. *Miami International Airport?*

Aware that Tobias could hear what she was saying, she walked a few more steps away and tried to keep her voice smooth and pleasant. "I need more details, Mike."

"Uh…sorry about breaking the news to you like this but, you know I was trying out for that soap?

Well, thing is, someone put in a good word for me, and I got a part. Not the lead, but who knows? Now that I'm in, the *sky's* the limit—"

"Mike."

"So, yeah. I need to be in LA tomorrow—"

A feminine voice cut Mike off, followed by a loud rustling, as if Mike was attempting to cover the speaker end of the phone.

Although muffled, Allegra distinctly heard his muttered, "Felicity, babe, just give me some space for a minute? I'm talking to, you know, *her.*"

Felicity. That would be one of the girls Mike shared an apartment with and who Allegra had thought was just a good friend. Clearly, they were a whole lot friendlier than he had let on.

"Let's cut this short," Allegra said crisply. "You've got some kind of acting part. Now, you're flying somewhere with a *friend*—"

"Felicity, yeah. We're leaving for LA. Like, right now."

Allegra frowned, sudden suspicion gnawing at her. Mike was broke, he had told her so, and she hadn't yet paid him for being her fake fiancé. That was one of the things she was going to address this afternoon. So where did he get the money to pay for flights to LA, not only for himself, but for Felicity? It was possible the production had paid him an advance, but it was a small part, and he had only just heard this morning. Added to that his departure was so sudden, and *organized* when, normally, Mike couldn't organize his way out of a paper bag, that she didn't see how any of it was possible.

Suspicion coalesced into knowledge. Mike had failed to make their date; instead, *Tobias* had turned up. "When, exactly, did Tobias buy the tickets?"

There was a small horrified silence. "How did you *know*?"

Allegra's jaw tightened. "The same way I know he was the one who 'put a good word in for you,' probably with one of the financial backers. So, when? Yesterday, or this morning?"

The timing made a difference, because, if Tobias had arranged to get rid of Mike last night, before they had slept together, that would make his actions in sleeping with her even more calculated.

"This morning. He got in contact with someone in LA. An hour later, the production manager offered me the part. Tobias was totally cool. He paid for our tickets, even arranged accommodation—"

"And your job at the spa?"

A final boarding call echoed in the background, cut through by Felicity's terse statement that she was boarding now, even if Mike wasn't.

"Yeah, sorry about that," Mike mumbled. "I sent an email, like, ten minutes ago. Look, I gotta go—"

The call terminated.

Allegra flicked through to her emails and opened Mike's resignation, which barely extended to two lines, one of them being, *Hi, Ms Mallory*.

She closed the email and slipped her phone back into her tote. Grimly, she noted that her strategy with

Mike had worked, after a fashion. Tobias had reacted in a possessive, macho way, but not as she had hoped.

Instead of expressing an interest in having a real relationship, where they dated and got to know one another, *like he had done with Francesca*, he had behaved in the exact opposite way. He had gotten rid of the "threat" Mike had posed by buying him off and shipping him to the other side of the country. And there was only one way Mike would have suddenly gotten a part in the production; Tobias had also paid for that.

As if he had never heard of fighting for the woman he wanted by courting her.

Instead, he had been one step ahead of her, clearing the way so he could have unimpeded access to her for the next month.

His actions were ruthless and definitively alpha, and they informed her that Tobias really did want the sex, enough that he had been prepared to pay for it.

If she hadn't had the state of their "relationship" pointed out to her by the way he was with Francesca, maybe she would have been thrilled by the fact that he had been prepared to go to such lengths to get her to himself.

But, the plain fact was, he had inexcusably changed the rules. Just over two years ago, she had fended off two wealthy men who thought she could be bought with money, gifts and influence.

She hadn't been selling herself then, and she wasn't doing it now.

Jaw set, Allegra dropped her phone into her bag,

made an executive decision and walked. On the way, she saw a cleaner mopping up something that had been spilled on the floor, so she stopped and handed her the bouquet of roses.

Holding a bunch of flowers, that looked like they had been bought for her by a lover, now only seemed to symbolize what was *not* in her future. They represented the romantic aspects of a relationship, which Tobias had once very publicly extended to Francesca, but which he had *never* extended to her.

As if all he truly wanted from her *was* the sex.

Tobias saw the moment Allegra turned on her heel and headed for the elevators.

Suddenly over Francesca and her friend, and the incessant girl-talk, he said a clipped goodbye and strode toward the elevators.

At a guess, Allegra had just gotten a call from Callaghan. From the way she had reacted, she knew he'd gotten rid of him.

That meant that either Callaghan had crumbled and blurted out that Tobias had arranged to move him to the West Coast, or she had extracted the information.

He was betting on the second option.

Allegra stepped into the elevator. Her gaze, which was definitely frosty, clashed with his as he stopped the doors from closing with a hand and stepped in with her. "We were in the middle of a conversation."

"Were we? I hardly noticed."

"We were talking about a relationship."

"There's a big difference between the kind of interaction you call a relationship, and what I want." Her dark eyes shot fire. "You paid Mike off!"

A little grimly, he wondered how those two statements fitted together. "I got rid of Mike so we could *have* a relationship."

The elevator stopped at a floor; the doors slid open.

Allegra jabbed a finger at his chest. "You're *paying* for sex!"

There was a small, vibrating silence as an elderly couple, who were waiting for the elevator, stared at them as if they'd each grown an extra head.

Tobias nodded in their direction, took Allegra's arm and hurried her out of the elevator. "How in hell am I paying for sex?"

She jerked free of his hold. "How much did it cost to get rid of Mike?"

He quoted the six figures it had cost him so the producer could be convinced that Callaghan could handle a small part.

She gave him a horrified look. "They make movies about this stuff."

"I just did what worked. Now, tell me how that equates to me paying to have sex with you?"

She met his gaze squarely. "Simple accounting. You've bankrolled Mike's acting career to get me into bed, so now it's almost as if you've paid to have sex with me. You've *commoditized* our relationship."

"I don't see it that way," he said bluntly. "We slept together last night. As far as I was concerned, you *al-*

ready belonged to me, so why would I pay for what's already mine? I got rid of Callaghan because he's a guy. If he had tried to touch you, I would have had to deck him."

She stared at him for long seconds, her eyes oddly dark. "You really do want me."

"It's a little more than that." Tobias steered her in the direction of the parking lot. "Like I said before, I wanted to talk about a relationship."

Allegra drove with care through the rain, which was steady now. The clouds above were dark and heavy-bellied, but the temperature was still warm enough that steam wisped off roads and sidewalks. The traffic was thick, but she was still intensely aware that Tobias was once again tailing her, although, this time, she felt entirely different about it. Instead of feeling ruffled and on edge, excited waves of pleasure kept zinging through her.

Tobias wanted a relationship with her. Finally, he was seeing her as "the prize."

She turned into the long driveway to the mansion, hit the garage remote and parked jerkily in her space. Weirdly, she was actually nervous, and felt all thumbs as she grabbed her key. Tobias's black truck glided to a halt beside her convertible.

Her tension ratcheted up another notch as she climbed out from behind the wheel and reached over to grab the tote, but, as she did so, Tobias pulled her into his arms and kissed her, his mouth warm against hers.

Dimly, she registered that she'd let the tote drop onto the driver's seat and, because the door was still open, it had then overbalanced and tumbled onto the garage floor. But, in that moment, nothing mattered but the relief that, finally, Tobias was kissing her.

But, before they made love again, she needed the answer to the questions that had gnawed at her. Planting her palms on his chest, she pushed free. "Francesca Messena?"

He frowned. "What about her?"

"You dated her before you slept with me two years ago, then you dated her afterward. In fact, you *pursued* her—"

"I didn't pursue her," he growled. "Why would I? She's not my type."

It wasn't the answer she expected. It was blunt, male and irritable, but it made her happier than any other answer could. She stared at him for a long, silent moment, because this was *important*. "Am I your type?"

His brows jerked together. "Is this some kind of trick question?"

"No tricks."

A rueful smile quirked the corner of his mouth. "After six years? Babe, you know you are."

She tried not to dance on the spot. "Okay, last question. What kind of relationship, exactly, do you want to talk about?"

"A real one," he said flatly. "I want you with me, so no other guy can get near you. We'll argue, because we're both strong-headed, but, the way I see it, even though things aren't perfect, we stay together and figure it out."

She blinked. Those words could have come out of her own mouth. "Okay. Where did the aliens take the *real* Tobias?"

He grinned, and Allegra stared at him, suddenly transfixed and almost too happy. But, at the same time, there was a peculiar tension at the back of her mind, because it all seemed too quick and easy. Twice, things had gone wrong, so she couldn't quite believe it was going to be smooth sailing this time around.

She drew a deep breath."Okay. Let's try. That sounds good to me."

Lifting up on her toes, she angled her jaw and kissed him. It had been a long, horrible day. She had been anxious, miserable and on edge, and she had thought she had lost Tobias.

Tobias responded by lifting her up, cupping her bottom as he held her against him. Dimly, she registered that they were walking. He set her down as he opened the door that led to the house, linked his fingers with hers, then led her into the hallway that ran past the kitchen.

They didn't make it to the upstairs bedroom. Instead, Tobias swung her into his arms, carried her several steps, then shouldered into a downstairs guest room. White shutters cut out the gloom of the rainy afternoon, throwing shadows over the large white bed.

Setting her down on her feet, he shrugged out of

his jacket, dragged off his tie, then pulled her close again. When she surfaced from the kiss, she fumbled at his buttons, pulled at the crisp, gauzy linen until it slid from his shoulders, then slid her palms over hard muscle and heated skin.

Another languorous kiss, and she registered the loosening of her skirt as the zipper glided down. Cool air circulated against her skin as turquoise silk puddled on the floor. She pulled free to undo the shirt, which was tied, then lifted it over her head, along with the soft camisole. Moments later, her bra was gone, and her breath came in as Tobias cupped her breasts, bent down and took one nipple into his mouth.

Sensation shimmered and seared, tension rocketed through her, then they were moving again, backward this time. She felt the brush of cool cotton on the back of her thighs. Then, she pulled at the fastening of his pants, dragged the zipper down and cupped him.

Tobias muttered something short and flat, stilled her hand and pulled her close for another deep, drugging kiss. Seconds later, he peeled out of his pants, then paused to extract a foil packet from the pocket. Breath locked in her throat, she stepped out of her own panties and climbed onto the bed, watching as he tore open the packet and sheathed himself. Moments later, he joined her on the bed, but, as he settled himself between her legs, she pushed at his shoulders.

"Not this way."

He grinned and allowed her to push him on his back, then straddle him and slowly sheath herself.

His hands settled at her hips and, she began to move, a little awkwardly at first, then with growing confidence. His gaze locked with hers as he reached up and cupped her breasts. She gasped as tension coiled and gathered. A split second later, Tobias moved, reversing their positions and holding her beneath him as he slowly thrust inside her. Long minutes passed, during which she clung to his shoulders. Despite the rain, the afternoon was warm, the air thick and humid, making it difficult to breathe. Reaching up, she pulled his head down and fastened her mouth to his, and the afternoon splintered and shimmered into sultry heat.

Half an hour later, Allegra woke from a light doze and immediately knew something was wrong.

Tobias, dressed only in just his narrow, dark suit pants, his chest bare, was standing in the doorway, one hand filled with expensive, luxurious diamonds. His remote gaze, when it had been so soft and warm before, struck a chill through her. "Where did you get these?"

Allegra sat up straight, dragging the sheet around her breasts. She had been relaxed and warm, but now her stomach was tight and churning, her mind whirling a million miles an hour. Tobias must have gone out to the garage and seen her tote on the floor. At a guess, the case of diamonds had tumbled out and opened. "I think that's my business, but if you must know, the diamonds came from Esmae. They're Mallory family jewelry."

He was silent for a beat. "Try again, Allegra. Everyone knows Esmae was broke before she married my grandfather. Apparently, she had a few Edwardian trinkets, but nothing of any value."

The shock of the words, the way they were said, was like a slap in the face.

Out of nowhere, her heart began to race. Allegra drew a quick breath. "Okay then," she said quietly, "you tell me where I got them from."

"I know about the scandal in San Francisco."

And he was putting two and two together: supposed lovers, gifts of expensive jewelry. "Of course. That's why you ditched me two years ago, so I suppose it's just as good an excuse to ditch me now."

His brows jerked together. "This is not about ditching."

She noticed he didn't refute that he had dumped her because he had bought into Halliday's and Fischer's lies. "So you still want to sleep with me, despite everything?"

She cut him off before he could answer. "If you want to know where the necklace came from, you could always get your little detective, Tulley, to do some more legwork." Her stomach sank when she logged the expression on his face. "Too late. You've already gotten him to pry into my past."

"Only because it didn't add up."

"Of course, it didn't. It's hard to trace where pretty women get their jewelry from, especially when it's given to them by their families or as pageant prizes, or from an elderly aunt. But if you need verification, call a jeweler called Clark who works at Ambrosi. He's doing some checking for me on provenance and value. By now, he should have the record of sale for the pieces that came from Esmae. As for the rest of the diamonds I own, where I got them from is private and absolutely none of your business."

Tobias frowned. "I had to ask—"

"I know. But if you don't mind," she said coolly, winding the sheet around herself like a toga, and stepping out of the bed. "I need to get dressed and get back to work. It's the middle of the afternoon and, now that Mike's gone, we're short-staffed."

Tobias stared at her. For a moment, she almost thought he was going to soften, take her in his arms and say he was sorry for doubting her. That he didn't care where the diamonds came from, and that the only thing that mattered was what they felt for one another.

But then his phone rang, breaking the moment. Placing the jewels onto the dressing table, he slid his phone out of his back pocket and left the room, closing the door behind him.

Allegra stared at the door. She had managed to hide it, but the fact that Tobias had had her investigated, and that he still refused to take her word, had shaken her.

She guessed that, in her heart of hearts, she had hoped he would finally let his stubborn distrust of her go, that if she poured enough love into the relationship, he would understand *who* she was, and allow himself to fall for her.

She had been wrong.

Allegra collected the diamonds, her jaw tightening at the way Tobias had so easily reverted to seeing her as the kind of shallow, cliché woman who would exchange sex for jewelry.

She had zero tolerance for that kind of stereotyping. In Tobias's case: less than zero.

Added to that, she was over the idea that Esmae had married for money and that Mallory women bartered relationships for a cushy lifestyle.

She knew something of Tobias's background, that the narrative was reinforced by his own experience as a child, when his father had lavished jewelry on his mistresses, but it didn't make it any easier to hear. It threw up the barrier that had been standing between them all along: that Tobias didn't seem to trust in love.

And he especially didn't trust in *her love.*

Her problem was, she was in love with Tobias, and had been for six years. However, she was now certain that love was not something Tobias would probably ever feel for her. How could he, when he clearly didn't trust her?

The grim line in Elena Lyons-Messena's book seemed to flash like a neon light in her mind.

If your alpha shows no signs of falling in love, leave. Save yourself.

She had to leave. Today.

She couldn't stay. Not in Tobias's bed, or even this

house. She would lose her shares, but she didn't care, she preferred to keep her self-respect. It just meant that she would do what she should always have done, and buy Tobias out.

As for the clause in the will that said her oldest brother Quin could make some kind of claim should Tobias not manage the resort for the full month, she would tell Quin to stay out of it, and she would tell him why. Once he understood what was at stake, he would take her side. Family was family.

It would be a wrench leaving. It was going to hurt way more than it had two years ago, because now she knew she was in love with Tobias, and had been all along. But she could not stay with a man who did not trust her.

She had kept herself on hold for Tobias for six years, and the plain fact was she couldn't afford to do that anymore.

Opening the door, she headed for the stairs. The low timbre of Tobias's voice registered somewhere in the distance, which only made her feel more miserable, because she had gotten used to the sound of his voice, and used to having him near.

Worried about her heart rate, Allegra phoned her doctor and made an urgent appointment. Afterward, she quickly showered and dressed, choosing a pair of natural-colored linen pants, a white camisole and, because it was definitely cooling down, a white sweater. Moving like an automaton she fixed a pair of silver filigree earrings that were go-to favorites to her lobes and applied basic makeup.

As she coiled her hair into a loose knot and pinned it, she noted that her heart was still pounding too fast. Worryingly, it hadn't stopped, and it was starting to make her feel light-headed.

She strapped on her sports watch, tapped the app on her phone and waited for the reading to come up. The rate was one hundred and thirty beats per minute. She would routinely achieve that when she was doing a workout, but all she was doing was strolling around her bedroom.

Not good.

It was possible the rate would drop, and this was nothing but a false alarm. However, just in case she did need to go to the hospital, she packed a change of underwear, some jeans and a casual sweatshirt in her tote. On the two occasions she had been admitted, the first had been an overnight stay, and the second had amounted to just a couple of hours. She had no idea what would happen this time, but she needed to be prepared to stay overnight. Both times chemical intervention had worked its magic and switched her heart rate back to a normal rhythm.

The decision to leave Tobias, now, before she went to the doctor, settled in. She was twenty-seven; thirty was just around the corner, and the speed with which the years were passing was getting scary.

Marriage and babies had not been at the forefront of her thinking. How could they be, when she had never been able to settle into a viable relationship because she had been hopelessly in love with a man who had no conception of who she truly was?

The plain fact was, she *did* want love and marriage. And she wanted them with a man who could truly love and cherish her.

And that man was not Tobias.

Fourteen

Feeling slightly shaky with adrenaline, Allegra retrieved her suitcase from the closet and began tossing clothes into it. She snatched a Messena jungle-print dress off the hanger, gathered up lingerie, marched out to the bedroom and shoved it all in the suitcase.

Feeling increasingly agitated, *because she had spent so much money on buying Francesca-lookalike things*, she gathered up shoes and packed them into a separate bag. By the time she had packed all of her clothes, the case was stuffed full of Messena pieces. She needed to weed them out, give them away and concentrate on getting herself back.

Not that she had lost herself, she thought grimly. All she had lost was her confidence.

Walking through to the bathroom, she packed her

toiletries. Returning to the bedroom, she shoveled her makeup into a carry case, cleared out the dresser and zipped her suitcase closed.

Feeling distinctly breathless, because the rushing around had made her heart race even faster, she snapped the jewelry cases closed and dropped them into her tote. On impulse, she also stored Alexandra's diary in her tote. If she was going to have some downtime in the hospital, or even at home, she might as well read it.

The sound of a door closing brought her head up. It could only be Tobias, because it was late enough that Marta would have left for the day. For a moment, she thought he might stop at her door and knock, but he continued past. She heard his tread on the stairs, then the closing of the kitchen door.

The sound of his truck starting was only just audible through the rain, which had gotten heavier. Bleakly, Allegra slipped into comfortable flats. The weather was supposed to deteriorate more, with strong winds and heavy rain, so there was no point wearing delicate high heels.

Ten minutes later, she had all of her luggage jammed into her cramped convertible. She started the car and activated the soft top. When it was snugly in place, she backed out. It was still too early for her appointment with her doctor, so she decided to drive to her apartment and unload the luggage first.

As she accelerated down the drive, which was already littered with leaves stripped off by the blustery winds, she speed-dialed Janice and told her that she was very possibly on her way to hospital for the afternoon, and asked her to go through their list of part-time therapists and see who was available to come in and take over Mike's classes for the rest of the week.

An hour later, after dropping off her things at her apartment, and the consult with her doctor, she phoned Janice who knew some basics about her condition, and told her she was being admitted to Mercy Hospital, probably just for the afternoon. Luckily, her doctor, Alicia Ortez, had worked at Mercy for a number of years and had been able to get her a referral direct to the cardiac unit rather than sending her to sit in the ER. That wasn't exactly usual practice but, because Esmae had left Mercy a sizable donation in her will, *and* there was a bed available for a few hours, Allegra had gotten seen. And, happily, she could afford Mercy. One of the things her parents had done for her was make sure she had excellent medical insurance.

As familiar as she was with the process after two previous admissions, the procedure was still slightly scary—after all, this was her *heart*. After she'd had her pulse and blood pressure checked by a nurse, she was transferred to a room and hooked up to an electrocardiogram. Half an hour later, a doctor strolled in, checked her stats and asked her a list of questions about what might have kicked off this episode.

The phrase *a broken heart* popped into her mind. But, when her pulse jumped and she saw his frown, she took a slow, deep breath, attempted to exude calm serenity, and mentioned Esmae's death and the stress of work. He ticked a couple of boxes, hooked the clipboard on the end of her bed, then administered a drug she'd had before, Adenosine, which she knew acted to chemically reset the electrical activity of her heart.

If that didn't work, the next option was electrical cardioversion, which she would only agree to as an absolute last resort. It was bad enough knowing that the drug he was injecting would slow, even pause, her heart in order to reset the rate. Allegra did not want to have the job done with who knew however many volts of electricity.

While she waited for the drug to work, she picked up her phone, which she'd set on her bedside table, and turned it off. Janice knew where she was, and why, so there was no need to be in touch. And the last thing she needed right now was to unconsciously wait for Tobias to call her, then start *hoping* that he would. That was the kind of thinking that had worked against her for the past six years.

Instead, she reached for Alexandra's diary and began to read.

An hour later, she set it down.

The story Alexandra had written in her own hand had been intensely personal and unexpected. She had had an affair with Jebediah, but it hadn't just been an affair; they *had* planned to marry. At a guess, the engagement ring Allegra had had resized that morning had been Alexandra's engagement ring from Jebediah.

Unfortunately, Alexandra's husband, a wealthy

and powerful English aristocrat who had a reputation for violence, and who they all thought had died before Alexandra had left England, hadn't died at all. Intent on reclaiming his runaway wife, he had travelled to America, and had found out where she lived. Warned by her lawyer, Alexandra had taken the children and run.

She had settled in New York, hoping to lose herself in the city, but he had eventually found her there, too, and had claimed her house and all her assets. True to form, he had put Alexandra in hospital, then had gone back to England, leaving her broke.

But he hadn't gotten everything. Knowing the risk, Alexandra had systematically converted the oil money into diamonds, an investment she had buried in the garden of the townhouse that had just been sold from under her. Just before she died of her injuries, she had directed Esmae to dig up the jewelry, sell half of it and give the cash to her son, Allegra's grandfather. Esmae was to sell whatever diamonds she needed to live, but to keep as many as possible as insurance against hard times.

But Esmae had clearly been luckier in love than Alexandra had ever been, which explained why she had managed to keep a great deal of Alexandra's jewelry, and why she hadn't ever worn it. In honor of Alexandra, she had kept it hidden away, an "insurance policy" she had then passed on to Allegra.

Tobias strode into his downtown office and dropped his briefcase on his desk. He closed his door, signaling to his PA that he wanted privacy. The last thing he needed was for Jean to be privy to the calls he was about to make.

He had spent the last hour surfing the social media accounts of both Halliday and Fischer, so, when he got hold of Tulley, it was no surprise to hear what he had to report.

Both men had unsavory reputations and a bent for going after younger women. The evidence pointed to Burns-Stein Halliday failing to act on Allegra's behalf because Halliday was the nephew of one of the partners and Fischer was married to the senior partner's daughter. The kicker was, that this wasn't the first time they had covered up for Fischer and Halliday.

Tobias thanked Tulley and hung up. He walked over to his large picture window, which looked out across city buildings to the sea. The wind velocity had gone up, even in the short time he had been in the office, and the rain had come in, turning the city gray, but that wasn't what concerned him.

Allegra had endured a major injustice in her life yet, with all the online hype Fischer and Halliday had generated, he had never heard so much as a whisper of the actual facts. And Allegra had never chosen to confide in him.

And why would she, he thought bleakly, when she must have known that he'd been only too happy to buy into the wrong story.

Collecting his briefcase, he took the elevator down to the street, then a cab to the Atraeus Mall. Minutes later, he walked into Ambrosi. The jeweler Allegra had mentioned, Clark, confirmed that Allegra had phoned to request that he give Tobias the same information regarding provenance that he had given her.

Tobias studied the two sheets Clark handed him. They each had only one record of sale, to Alexandra Mallory. The name Faberge leaped off the first page. The current estimate for the necklace alone was seven figures.

Faberge. It was not the kind of jewelry that men like Halliday and Fischer handed out as gifts. It was investment jewelry. The kind families bought to hedge their wealth. He should know—his grandfather had bought enough of it.

Thanking Clark, he walked back through the mall.

As he walked, the consequences of his actions settled in. The second he had seen the diamonds and felt their weight, he had been flung back in time to the arguments that had used to rage between his parents, mostly about the jewelry his father had lavished on mistresses. Then he had remembered the online scandal around Allegra accepting jewelry for sex and the ground had seemed to shift beneath his feet.

He didn't want to accept that Allegra had been untruthful; he had thought he knew her through and through but, in those moments, he had wondered if he had let lust, and emotion, cloud his judgment. He had wondered if he had been fooled.

He now knew that he had jumped to a completely wrong conclusion. He had let his own trust issues, and the knee-jerk jealousy that had gripped him because it seemed that she *had* slept with Fischer and Halliday, cloud his judgment.

If he could kick himself, he would. As a mistake, it was unforgiveable.

He headed back out to the street, which was now teeming with rain, caught a cab and phoned Allegra while he was en route to his office building. When there was no reply, twice, he tried the spa's number.

Janice picked up. Allegra wasn't at the spa because she'd had to go to the hospital.

Tobias went cold inside. His first thought was that Allegra must have had some kind of accident. "What for?"

"Oh, it's that heart condition she has. It's got some weird name. She just calls it SVT. I don't think it's a major problem, though, since she drove herself to Mercy."

Tobias hung up. His heart was pounding. His mother had died from a heart condition that had come out of nowhere. He had been eighteen at the time, but he still remembered how that had felt.

The cab pulled into his office building. He paid the cab driver. Mercy Hospital was in Coconut Grove. That was about a fifteen-minute drive. He stepped into the elevator and punched in the parking garage. Before the doors opened, he had rung Mercy and was talking to Admissions, who confirmed Allegra was a patient in the cardiac unit.

By the time he had reached his truck, he had checked online, found a description for SVT and read the symptoms. There were ranges of severity and a variety of treatments, including shock treatment to reset the heart. Apparently, stress was often a factor in episodes.

Stomach tight, he swung behind the wheel, started the truck and accelerated toward the exit.

He had made a mistake in not believing Allegra's explanation about the jewelry. He had seen the shock on her face, the way she had lifted her hand to her heart. Now, because of him, she was in the hospital.

It spun him back two years, to a call he had gotten from Lindsay's father to let him know that she had miscarried their baby. A baby he hadn't even known existed. Brice Howell had made no bones about the fact that Tobias's actions in leaving Lindsay for another woman was the reason that baby had died.

He reached the hospital, bypassed Admissions and strode into the cardiology ward, only to find that he had missed Allegra by ten minutes.

Relief filled him. If she had walked out of the hospital, then she must be okay.

Minutes later, he finally got the conversation he needed to have with the doctor who had treated Allegra, and was stonewalled because he wasn't a relative. Although the doctor did inform him that her problem had been "resolved."

Tobias's jaw tightened as he stepped out of the shelter of the hospital foyer into the now-pouring rain. The doctor refusing to talk to him about Allegra's condition, *because he was neither her husband nor her partner*, had struck him forcibly.

That was going to change.

He had messed up, big time. But that wouldn't happen again. *If* she let him back into her life, he would ensure she had the best medical attention. From now on, if Allegra had so much as a paper cut, then he needed to know about it. If she had a medical emergency, he would be there. He would carry her around on a silk cushion, if that was what worked.

By the time he reached his truck and swung behind the wheel, he was soaked.

Dragging off his wet jacket and tie, he tossed them onto the back seat. His shirt was plastered to his skin in places, but that barely registered. As he merged into traffic, he rang Allegra's phone and, again, got no reply.

He didn't think she would go to work, since it was so late in the afternoon, but, at that point, he wasn't about to let any detail slip, so he dialed Janice again.

When Janice confirmed that she hadn't heard from Allegra since she had phoned to let her know she was going to Mercy, Tobias terminated the call. He tried Allegra's number one more time, then concentrated on driving.

He switched on the local radio station, which was broadcasting a storm warning. Apparently, the hurricane that was supposed to veer into the Gulf was now going to hit Miami full on. Even though it was only five o'clock, the light was already murky, so he switched on his lights.

Heavy gusts of wind buffeted the truck as he

headed for Esmae's house. If Allegra wasn't there, he would drive to her apartment.

Whatever it took, he would find her.

Fifteen

Allegra arrived at Esmae's house. She hadn't wanted to come back, but, while she was in the hospital, she had remembered the painting she had left in the beach house. After reading the diary, and everything that had gone wrong for Alexandra, there was no way she was going to leave that behind.

As she parked out on the drive, she noticed that Jose, Marta's husband, had already been there and had closed the storm shutters over the windows of the house. There were no lights on inside, so it didn't look like Tobias was home.

Stepping out of her car, she jogged down to the beach house. Even though she was wearing a rain jacket, her jeans were instantly soaked. When she reached the cottage, the wind was even stronger, whipping the sea into a frenzy and filling the air with a misty, salty brine that stung her eyes.

She noted that Jose had missed one of the shutters on the beach house, so she attempted to close it, then gave up when she realized the bolt was broken. Muttering beneath her breath, she had to leave it.

Dragging wet strands of hair from her face, she made her way around the deck, holding onto the rails to anchor herself. It was then that she saw the dinghy, which was attached by a rope looped around a bollard at the end of the short pier.

In his rush to get the house and the beach cottage secured, Jose had obviously forgotten about putting the dinghy out of harm's way in the boathouse. Normally, it was safe enough to be left bobbing lazily at the end of the pier, but, with the combination of a high tide and the storm surge that was supposed to be coming, it was in danger of being smashed against the pier or swept away altogether.

Leaning into the wind, Allegra walked quickly down the steps to the beach and onto the wet pier. Grasping the side rail, she made her way, step by careful step, to the end. Clinging to the rail with one hand, she went down on her hands and knees to lessen resistance to the wind, and began working at the knot that secured the dinghy.

A wave broke, drenching her with spray. Dashing water from her eyes, she resumed working at the soaked rope, but it kept getting pulled tight by the wind and waves, which were dragging at the dinghy.

To ease the tension, she leaned forward and

grabbed the rope in order to haul the dinghy in closer and create some slack. She almost had the knot undone when the sound of her name being called jerked her head around. A small shock went through her when she saw Tobias, his face like thunder, as he roared at her to leave the dinghy.

In that moment, another wave broke, this one bigger than the last, surging over the jetty itself. Her feet went from under her. With a yelp, she tried to maintain her grasp on the rail. The plan was to drag herself upright and hook one arm around so she could haul herself back up, but the wood was slippery, and the power of the water tore her hands loose.

Something, probably the dinghy, caught her a glancing blow on the side of the head as she was swept over the side of the jetty, then she hit the water.

Even though she was wet through, the coldness of the water was a shock.

Her first thought was that she had to get away from the pier itself, because she didn't want to be dashed against the enormous oyster-encrusted poles that supported it. The other danger was the dinghy, which was being flung back and forth by the wind and waves.

Surfacing dangerously close to the dinghy, she gulped a lungful of air and began to swim away from both the pier and the dinghy, which meant out to sea. Even though she was a strong swimmer, it was hard to make headway in the lumpy, turbulent water but, once she was a few yards clear, she could turn toward the shore.

Breathless, she treaded water for a moment and twisted around to get her bearings. A wave surged over her, driving her back in the direction of the shore, which would be a wonderful thing if only she wasn't still too close to the dinghy.

She swam another couple of strokes then braced for the next wave. This time when she came up gasping for air and coughing, because somehow she had managed to swallow some water, movement on the pier caught her eye.

Tobias. Soaked to the skin in a shirt and dark pants, he was gripping the railing, scanning the water. His gaze locked on hers.

Another wave surged but, this time, she was prepared. Duck-diving, she kicked smoothly through. When she bobbed up on the other side, the pier was empty. Fear spasmed in her chest. Tobias must have been caught by the wave. A split second later, he surfaced beside her. Then, there was no time to think as the next wave broke.

When she came up for air, Tobias's gaze locked with hers. "Are you okay to swim? We need to get to shore before this gets any worse."

The relief that had flooded her when Tobias had popped up beside her turned to an intoxicating flood of warmth, *because he had jumped in to rescue her.* "I can swim."

A few strokes, hampered by the lumpy waves, and she felt the bottom. As she straightened, a wave hit her in the back. Tobias's arm snaked around her middle, anchoring her against his side, and they waded the last few yards to shore. When they reached the hard-packed sand, already littered with driftwood and seaweed, he pulled her close, bent down and kissed her, his mouth hard against hers and tasting of salt.

When he lifted his head, his gaze blazed into hers. "I thought I'd lost you. What in hell were you doing in the water? Haven't you heard, there's a hurricane—"

"I was getting the dinghy—"

"If Jose asked you to get the dinghy, he's fired."

The roar of wind and waves seemed to drop away as she stared at the heated silver of his eyes, fringed by inky black lashes, the intriguing scar across his nose. "He didn't. He'd left before I got here."

"Which means it was all your idea. Why did I already know that?" He pulled her close again, his arms wrapping around her in a hug, which was somehow so much more intimate than the kiss had been.

Allegra wound her arms around his waist, soaking in the heat that radiated from him.

He lifted his head. "You almost gave me a heart attack."

"There wouldn't have been a problem if someone hadn't tied some kind of a weird knot, a million times too tight."

His expression turned wry. "You mean a standard boating knot, a round turn with two half hitches—"

"Whatever. It wouldn't budge."

"You shouldn't have been down here, period," he said flatly. "It's too damned dangerous. And you definitely shouldn't be out in a storm when you've just been discharged from the hospital."

Allegra went still inside. "How did you know about that?"

Tobias pulled her up the shore toward the beach house. "I've been trying to call you all afternoon. In the end, I rang Janice and she told me where you were—"

"You were *looking* for me?"

"No," he said grimly. "I was going *crazy* looking for you."

For a split second, she didn't know what to think or feel, then anger kicked in. She had thought they were finished. She had *grieved* over the loss. Now, suddenly, he was concerned about her—

"We need to get inside. The storm's supposed to peak in the next hour, and they're predicting a storm surge."

The pressurized whine of the wind seemed to lift a notch, as if the hurricane had just found another gear. Allegra glanced out to sea. It was becoming more turbulent by the minute, and visibility was fading as the mist thickened. "What about the dinghy—"

"Forget the dinghy. The way this storm's shaping up, we'll be lucky if the pier isn't washed away."

Tobias kept an arm locked around her waist, as if he couldn't bear to let her go, which was conflicting. Part of her wanted to bask in the happy glow that had started when he had jumped into the water to save her, the other part of her still wanted to fling all of her hurts in his face.

The wind buffeted them as they climbed the steps. Tobias leaned down to pick up a rain jacket he must have thrown down on his way to the pier. Allegra glanced back. The pier was now almost totally submerged. A shudder went through her at the shocking swiftness with which the water had risen, and how easily she had been swept over the side.

She gave Tobias a fierce look. "You shouldn't have jumped in."

"Worried about me?"

She caught his gaze and, for once, didn't bother trying to hide what she felt. Tobias was tough and strong, but the sea was savage. Regardless of how angry she was with him, how crazy he made her, the thought that something might happen to him made her go cold inside. "Yes."

He pulled her up the steps and into the protected lee of the beach house. Seconds later, he had the door open and held it against the wind as she stumbled inside.

Tobias slammed the door closed. The reduction in noise was a relief, even though the sound of the wind buffeting the cottage and the roar of the waves as they pounded the beach, was still frighteningly loud.

The hall was dim, courtesy of the shutters, which closed out almost all of the light. Tobias flicked on lights as they walked from the short hallway into the kitchen.

"You're bleeding. What have you done to your head?"

Allegra touched the side of her head and winced. The skin was broken, and she could already feel a small lump forming. "When I was washed off the pier, I think I caught the side of the dinghy."

Tobias brushed her hair aside, his fingers gentle as he examined the injury. "It's only a graze, but it needs antiseptic. And ice."

While she sat down at the kitchen table, he opened the fridge and found a tray of ice cubes, which he emptied into a clean kitchen towel. He handed her the makeshift ice pack, which she pressed to her head. He then disappeared in the direction of the bathroom. When he reappeared, he had a pile of fluffy white towels and a first aid kit.

The lights flickered as he dropped a towel around her shoulders, at which point she realized she was beginning to feel chilled. It wasn't cold, exactly, but the usual hot temperature had plunged, and her wet clothes were clinging to her.

Tobias pulled a chair close and sat down, his thighs bracketing hers as he opened the first aid kit and extracted a tube of antiseptic. "At least you can swim."

Allegra tried not to notice how mesmerizingly good Tobias looked with his light shirt plastered to the bronze glow of his skin. "Was that in your investigative report?"

His gaze caught hers. "I guess I deserved that. I used to watch you swimming off the beach. But, I admit, I also asked Esmae about you, and she told me you used to swim competitively."

He parted her hair and smeared on the antiseptic. "Although she failed to tell me that you had a heart condition, which makes what you did *even* worse—"

She jerked a little beneath his touch. "I didn't mean to end up in the water, and it's not really a heart condition. It's just a weird kind of electrical thing that happens, usually when I get overstressed."

Tobias stared at her for a long moment, an odd expression on his face, then he pushed to his feet, replaced the antiseptic in the first aid kit and started opening cupboard doors. The anger that had flowed through her, and the desire to be difficult, suddenly burned out, and she was left wishing for the warmth and intimacy they'd shared on the beach.

Picking up the ice pack, she settled it against her head again, and watched as he found coffee grounds and started making coffee. She noticed he had also placed a box of candles and a lighter on the kitchen counter, just in case the power went out. When the rich scent of dark roast filled the air as the machine began to drip coffee into the carafe, Tobias peeled off his wet shirt and dropped it over the back of a chair. Reaching for a towel, he dried himself off. When he was finished, he leaned on the counter and crossed his arms over his chest. "Why didn't you tell me about the SVT?"

Allegra dragged her gaze from his chest. "If you'll

remember, we didn't exactly spend a lot of time talking." Suddenly over being passive and looked after, she set the ice pack down on the table, pushed to her feet and began searching out mugs. "If you must know, I didn't tell you because I didn't think it would have mattered—"

"It mattered." Tobias's hand stayed hers as she set out sugar and teaspoons, and, suddenly, tension and a crazy nervousness were zinging through her.

Fingers threading with hers, he pulled her close. "I came looking for you because I knew I needed to fix what had happened this afternoon. Then, Janice told me you were in Mercy Hospital with a heart condition. I missed you at the hospital by a few minutes—"

He loosened his hold slightly. "When you walked out on me, I realized I'd made the same mistake in not trusting you that I'd been making all along." He hesitated. "Before I met you, you know I was involved with Lindsay."

"You were living together."

"For a couple of years. Lindsay wanted to get married. She wanted children, the whole deal. I agreed to marriage. She was already starting to plan the wedding, but, at that point, I knew it wouldn't work, so we broke up."

In terse words, he explained the difficulty he'd had with trust ever since his parents had broken up when he was ten. His father had had affairs then had left his mother to move in with an A-list party girl, the first in a long line, and his mother had become embittered.

"That's why I chose Lindsay," he said curtly. "I was looking for someone dependable and steady, mostly because I didn't want to be like my father. Then, I saw you on the beach and I fell like a ton of bricks. Combine that with the guilt I felt when I finally left Lindsay because I wanted you…"

He released her and walked over to the one window that wasn't protected by a shutter, and stared bleakly out at the storm. "But that wasn't the worst of it. I didn't know it, but apparently, when I left, she was pregnant. Not long after, she miscarried." He shrugged. "I went into damage control, and that meant denying that I wanted you."

A heavy gust of wind hit the beach house, making it creak, but she barely noticed the sound; she was still dealing with the shock of the revelation. "I'm so sorry you lost the baby," she said quietly. "When, exactly, did Lindsay miscarry?"

Tobias turned his head, his gaze oddly dark. "The day after you and I first slept together."

And, suddenly, it all made sense. She had always wondered why Tobias had dumped her cold, when the attraction between them had been so strong and it had felt so good to be together. Now, she knew: it had been the shock of loss, and guilt. "You blamed yourself for the miscarriage."

His expression was remote. "How could I not?"

Then, the online stories had reinforced his decision, ruining any chance of a relationship between them.

Even though it still made her feel angry and hurt,

it was time to address the scene in the guest bedroom that morning. "What about your reaction to the jewelry? I'm guessing you read some of the online lies Halliday and Fischer wrote about me."

His expression was bleak. "It hit some buttons, mostly because my father spent a small fortune on jewelry for his various 'friends' and I couldn't stand the thought that you might have slept with Fischer and Halliday. When I walked out to the garage and saw the new jewelry case and the jewels spilled across the seat of your car, I…reacted."

She took a deep breath. "Do you realize how much that *hurt*?"

Tobias crossed the space between them, cupped her shoulders and pulled her close. "Babe, I'm sorry I hurt you, and sorry it took me so long to acknowledge the truth. When you walked out on me, I nearly went crazy—"

They were suddenly plunged into darkness as the power flicked out.

Tobias muttered something beneath his breath. Seconds later, he had the first candle lit and positioned in a glass. Three more candles later, positioned at strategic points, and the kitchen was filled with the warm flickering glow.

The coffee machine had finished filtering, so he poured the coffee, spooned in sugar and handed her a hot mug. "You need to drink that," he said abruptly. "You look too damn pale."

She inhaled the rich aroma. There was no milk,

but she didn't care. Hot, sweet coffee when she was wet and chilled was ambrosia.

"There's something else we need to talk about," he said. "I got Tulley to investigate the two men who attempted to destroy your reputation."

Allegra's head jerked up at the way Tobias had framed his words, as if she was *innocent*. She winced a little, because the sudden movement made her head throb. "Why?"

"Because the online stories have nothing to do with who you are. And, as it turns out, those two particular men have unsavory reputations."

"And a lot of money and influence." She met his gaze squarely. "Fischer actually tried to seduce me in my office—"

Cold fury registered in Tobias's eyes, and a small shiver went down her spine. Suddenly, the fact that he had been a Special Forces soldier operating in some of the most violent and dangerous places on the planet was starkly evident.

"I'll kill him," he said softly.

"No need. I hit him with a stapler."

"You did *what*?"

"It was a big stapler." She didn't bother to hide the satisfaction in her voice. "He went down."

Amusement surfaced in Tobias's eyes. It was an odd moment to realize that, just when she had thought everything had fallen apart, he did something masculine and irresistibly *alpha* and, even though she knew he was dictatorial, terminally edgy and *difficult*, she wanted him back all over again.

"I know what they did to you," he growled. "That's why I sent Tulley to investigate them. He did some digging and came up with conclusive evidence that both Halliday and Fischer had been trolling on-line dating sites and misrepresenting themselves to women for years. There were also a couple of assault convictions that had been quashed, probably because the women had gotten threatened or paid off. To put it politely, their behavior was predatory."

He crossed his arms over his chest. "But, as it happens, Hunt Security and the various businesses the Messena and Atraeus families own, do some business with Burns-Stein Halliday. I emailed Burns the investigative report and suggested that if they continued to employ Halliday and Fischer, there would be repercussions. Also, that they needed to make reparations to you, ASAP, or I would be over there."

Her throat closed up, and, for a long moment, her breathing felt impeded. She had thought she had put it all behind her, that she had healed, but the pressure in her chest told her otherwise.

What had happened had *hurt*. She had thrown herself into study and work and then, practically overnight, it had all been taken from her in the most humiliating of ways.

When she could finally speak, her voice was husky. "What do you mean by *reparations*?"

"For a start, an apology. There's legislation about harassment in the workplace, and they ignored it. Then, there's the matter of compensation for your lost career—"

"I left voluntarily."

"You left because of what happened."

"I can't, exactly, afford to sue them—"

"Which is why *I'm* suing the ass off of them."

That shouldn't be romantic but it absolutely was, because Tobias had finally ridden to the rescue and was now *fighting* for her.

He was on her side, which meant Burns-Stein Halliday was toast. She would not want to be in their shoes if Tobias actually had to go over there. But she would definitely want to be in the room. "When you go, I'm coming with you."

His brows jerked together. "You're not going back to work for those clowns. You've got a great business right here and, as far as I'm concerned, for as long as you want them, the premises at the resort are yours."

A delicious glow of warmth started in her chest. Tobias was being commanding in a totally male, sexy way. Normally, as she had said before, she didn't take orders, but she would take this one because she was in complete agreement with it, and she totally loved that he was intent on protecting her. "Why would I go back to BSH? It would be like redoing the beauty pageant thing. I liked the pageants, and I liked winning, but then I got over them, and they just weren't my thing—"

"Babe, you're losing me."

She gave him a patient look. "The point is, I liked getting the degree, I liked the study and the achievement, but I didn't get the degree so I could work for Satan."

Tobias lifted a hand to his mouth to conceal the fact that he was laughing, although that was a pointless exercise, since his shoulders were shaking. "I assume you mean Burns—"

"That's right. Satan. I don't even know why you asked the question. And, back to that other thing you said about the lease… Since I'm perfectly happy in Miami, plus I'm beginning to think I've finally gotten a boyfriend, of course I'll be staying."

An emotion flashed in his gaze that made her heart stumble.

He muttered something short and flat and did what she was aching for him to do… Reaching her in one stride, he took her mug out of her hands, set it on the table, then hauled her into his arms.

They were both still damp and salty, they needed showers and fresh clothing, but Allegra was loath to give up these moments. She wanted to hold onto Tobias because, despite everything that had been said, a kernel of fear still existed that this newfound intimacy could vanish. "I wish I could have known all of those things about your relationship with Lindsay two years ago."

"Ditto to knowing about Halliday and Fischer," Tobias said somberly. Then, he rested his forehead on hers, which was totally cute. "We didn't know… but I'm pretty sure someone else did."

"Esmae."

"She knew I'd fallen for you."

And, in that moment, Allegra's heart soared and happiness expanded inside her, warm and bright and intoxicating enough to make her feel just the tiniest bit giddy. And not in a *get-to-the-hospital-for-drugs* kind of way.

She tipped her head back so she could study the lean contours of his face, the tough set of his jaw. "Fallen?" she probed, just to be doubly, positively sure.

Tobias's mouth quirked. "As in totally, head over heels, in love."

A slow smile spread across her face. "Just the way I am with you." She felt like dancing, like doing a victory lap, but she settled for hugging him hard and close.

He bent to kiss her. By the time he lifted his mouth, Allegra was clinging to his shoulders, soaking in his warmth and the steady thud of his heart. "I can hardly believe this is happening. It feels like a dream."

Tobias reached over to the back of a chair, where he'd tossed his jacket, and pulled a small jewelry box from the side pocket. "We can make it even more real. That is, if you'll say yes."

He opened the case, which bore the Ambrosi crest, and took out a solitaire diamond engagement ring that was breathtakingly beautiful in its simplicity. White fire glittered in the flickering light.

"It's beautiful."

"And it's brand new," he said flatly. "No history attached."

She drew a swift breath. *Now* it was real. "You bought it for me."

Tobias went down on one knee. "Allegra Mallory, will you marry me and be my love?"

There was only one answer she could give.

"Yes, yes and *yes*."

She held out her hand so he could slide the ring onto her finger and, as he did so, tears burned at the back of her eyes, but this time they were tears of joy.

Finally, she and Tobias had their happy ending.

* * * * *

Don't miss connected books in
The Pearl House series from Fiona Brand!

A Breathless Bride
A Tangled Affair
A Perfect Husband
The Fiancée Charade
Just One More Night
Needed: One Convenient Husband
Twin Scandals

WE HOPE YOU ENJOYED
THIS BOOK FROM
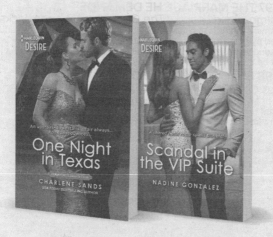

⬡ HARLEQUIN
DESIRE

*Luxury, scandal, desire—welcome to
the lives of the American elite.*

Be transported to the worlds of oil barons, family dynasties,
moguls and celebrities. Get ready for juicy plot twists,
delicious sensuality and intriguing scandal.

6 NEW BOOKS AVAILABLE EVERY MONTH!

COMING NEXT MONTH FROM

HARLEQUIN
DESIRE

Available April 13, 2021

#2797 THE MARRIAGE HE DEMANDS
Westmoreland Legacy: The Outlaws by Brenda Jackson
Wealthy Alaskan Cash Outlaw has inherited a ranch and needs land owned by beautiful, determined Brianna Banks. She'll sign it over with one condition: Cash fathering the child she desperately wants. But he won't be an absentee father and makes his own demand...

#2798 BLUE COLLAR BILLIONAIRE
Texas Cattleman's Club: Heir Apparent • by Karen Booth
After heartbreak, socialite Lexi Alderidge must focus on her career, not another relationship. But she makes an exception for the rugged worker at her family's construction site, Jack Bowden. Sparks fly, but is he the man she's assumed he is?

#2799 CONSEQUENCES OF PASSION
Locketts of Tuxedo Park • by Yahrah St. John
Heir to a football dynasty, playboy Roman Lockett is used to getting what he wants, but one passionate night with Shantel Wilson changes everything. Overwhelmed by his feelings, he tries to forget her—until he learns she's pregnant. Now he vows to claim his child...

#2800 TWIN GAMES IN MUSIC CITY
Dynasties: Beaumont Bay • by Jules Bennett
When music producer Will Sutherland signs country's biggest star, Hannah Banks, their mutual attraction is way too hot...so she switches with her twin to avoid him. But Will isn't one to play games—or let a scheming business rival ruin everything...

#2801 SIX NIGHTS OF SEDUCTION
by Maureen Child
CEO Noah Graystone cares about business and nothing else. Tired of being taken for granted, assistant Tessa Parker puts in her notice—but not before one last business trip with no-strings seduction on the schedule. Can their six hot nights turn into forever?

#2802 SO RIGHT...WITH MR. WRONG
The Serenghetti Brothers • by Anna DePalo
Independent fashion designer Mia Serenghetti needs the help of Damian Musil—son of the family that has been feuding with hers for years. But when one hot kiss leads to a passion neither expected, what will become of these star-crossed lovers?

"Are you really going to sell the Blazing Frontier without
even taking the time to look at it? It's a beautiful place."

"I'm sure it is, but I have no need of a ranch, dude or
otherwise."

"I think you're making a mistake, Cash."

Cash lifted a brow. Normally, he didn't care what any
person, man or woman, thought about any decision he made,
but for some reason what she thought mattered.

It shouldn't.

What he should do was thank her for joining him for
lunch, and tell her not to walk back to Cavanaugh's office
with him, although he knew both their cars were parked there.
In other words, he should put as much distance between them
as possible.

I can't.

Maybe it was the way her luscious mouth tightened when
she was not happy about something. He'd picked up on it
twice now. Lord help him but he didn't want to see it a third
time. He'd rather see her smile, lick an ice cream cone or...
lick him.

He quickly forced the last image from his mind, but not before a hum of lust shot through his veins. There had to be a reason he was so attracted to her. Maybe he could blame it on the Biggins deal Garth had closed just months before he'd gotten engaged to Regan. That had taken working endless days and nights, and for the past year Cash's social life had been practically nonexistent.

On the other hand, even without the Biggins deal as an excuse, there was strong sexual chemistry radiating between them. He felt it but honestly wasn't sure that even at twenty-seven she recognized it for what it was.

That was intriguing, to the point that he was tempted to hang around Black Crow another day. Besides, he was a businessman, and no businessman would sell or buy anything without checking it out first. He was letting his personal emotions around Ellen cloud what was usually a very sound business mind.

"You are right, Brianna. I would be making a mistake if I didn't at least see the ranch before selling it. Is now a good time?"

The huge smile that spread across her face was priceless... and mesmerizing. When was the last time a woman, any woman, had this kind of effect on him? When he felt spellbound? He concluded that never had a woman captivated him like Brianna Banks was doing.

Don't miss what happens next in
The Marriage He Demands
by Brenda Jackson, the next book in her
Westmoreland Legacy: The Outlaws series!

Available April 2021 wherever
Harlequin Desire books and ebooks are sold.

Harlequin.com

Get 4 FREE REWARDS!

We'll send you 2 FREE Books plus 2 FREE Mystery Gifts.

Harlequin Desire books transport you to the world of the American elite with juicy plot twists, delicious sensuality and intriguing scandal.

FREE Value Over $20

YES! Please send me 2 FREE Harlequin Desire novels and my 2 FREE gifts (gifts are worth about $10 retail). After receiving them, if I don't wish to receive any more books, I can return the shipping statement marked "cancel." If I don't cancel, I will receive 6 brand-new novels every month and be billed just $4.55 per book in the U.S. or $5.24 per book in Canada. That's a savings of at least 13% off the cover price! It's quite a bargain! Shipping and handling is just 50¢ per book in the U.S. and $1.25 per book in Canada.* I understand that accepting the 2 free books and gifts places me under no obligation to buy anything. I can always return a shipment and cancel at any time. The free books and gifts are mine to keep no matter what I decide.

225/326 HDN GNND

Name (please print)

Address   Apt. #

City   State/Province   Zip/Postal Code

Email: Please check this box ☐ if you would like to receive newsletters and promotional emails from Harlequin Enterprises ULC and its affiliates. You can unsubscribe anytime.

Mail to the **Harlequin Reader Service:**
IN U.S.A.: P.O. Box 1341, Buffalo, NY 14240-8531
IN CANADA: P.O. Box 603, Fort Erie, Ontario L2A 5X3

Want to try 2 free books from another series? Call 1-800-873-8635 or visit www.ReaderService.com.